W9-CUJ-045

0000079459

The Deputy Sheriff
of Comanche County

The Gregg Press Western Fiction Series

Priscilla Oaks, Editor

The Deputy Sheriff of Comanche County
Edgar Rice Burroughs

with a new introduction by
Robert E. Morsberger

Gregg Press

A Division of G. K. Hall & Co., Boston, 1979

Basalt Regiona. ......
P. O. Box BB
Basalt, Colo. 81621

With the exception of the Introduction, this is a complete photographic reprint of a work first published in Tarzana, CA by Edgar Rice Burroughs, Inc. in 1940. The trim size of the original hardcover edition was 5⅛ by 7¾ inches.

Text copyright by Edgar Rice Burroughs, Inc.
Reprinted by arrangement with Edgar Rice Burroughs, Inc.
Introduction copyright © 1979 by Robert E. Morsberger

Frontmatter designed by Designworks, Inc. of Cambridge, Massachusetts

Printed on permanent/durable acid-free paper and bound in the United States of America.
Republished in 1979 by Gregg Press, A Division of G.K. Hall & Co., 70 Lincoln St., Boston Massachusetts 02111

First Printing, September 1979

Library of Congress Cataloging in Publication Data
Burroughs, Edgar Rice, 1875–1950.
    The deputy sheriff of Comanche County.

    (The Gregg Press western fiction series)
    Reprint of the 1st ed. published by Burroughs, Tarzana, Calif.
    Includes bibliographical refernces.
    I. Title.   II. Series: Gregg Press western fiction series.
PZ.B944De   1979   [PS3503.U687]   813'.5'2   79-16674
ISBN 0-8398-2578-1

Introduction

BETWEEN 1923 AND 1930, Edgar Rice Burroughs wrote four Western novels. He had started his career as a novelist in 1912, when he wrote the first volume in his Martian series, *A Princess of Mars* (1917), followed the same year by the completion of *Tarzan of the Apes* (1914); and his success with African and interplanetary adventures kept editors and readers clamoring for more. Burroughs was eager to oblige them. His special literary gift, which made him the father of popular American science fiction, was his endlessly fertile imagination which he used to create numerous exotic and romantic fantasy worlds. The Western, on the other hand, requires a considerable degree of realism, a detailed knowledge of riding, roping, ranching, or of the Army and Indian fighting, and certainly of the land itself. Burroughs was, in fact, more qualified to provide this sort of realism than many Western novelists, for he had actually worked in Idaho and Arizona in the 1890s, first as a cowboy, then as a cavalryman. Yet it was not until 11 years after he became an established novelist that he wrote his first Western, *The Bandit of Hell's Bend* (1925), and then only under prodding from his English publisher, Sir Algernon Methuen.

Despite his hesitation to work in a new direction, Burroughs found the Western a congenial genre. *The Bandit of Hell's Bend* has a conventional plot but is notable for presenting an authentic picture of Arizona ranch life in the 1880s, a gallery of colorful and often comic characters, and the flavor of frontier humor. It was serialized in 1924 and published in hardcover in 1925. In it, the Apache Indians make two brief appearances as a menace to the ranchers, and in a raid, they kill the heroine's father. Burroughs knew, however, that this was only one side of the story; and in two of his finest novels, *The War Chief* (1927; Gregg Press edition, 1978), and *Apache Devil* (1933; Gregg Press edition, 1978), he chronicled the last years of the Apache wars from the Indian point of view. The Apache novels were meticulously researched; not only do they present a scrupulously accurate picture of Apache life and culture, of desert warfare and survival, but they condemn with scathing irony the hypocrisy, greed, bigotry, and bloodthirstiness of so-called civilization and champion the self-reliant freedom of the Indians' so-called savagery.

Thus, despite a belated start, Burroughs produced three Westerns within four years and was doing some of his best work in the genre. Not only did the novels have a realism lacking in his fantastic fiction, but they offered more subtle and substantial characterizations, a vigorous use of vernacular dialogue, and a more relaxed and natural style.

In 1930, he began his fourth (and as it turned out, his final) Western. Despite the fact that the initial impetus for Burroughs to turn to the Western came from his British publisher, editors were less than enthusiastic about Burroughs Westerns, preferring his well-established jungle and interplanetary adventures. Donald Kennicott, editor of McCall's *Blue Book* and *Red Book*, which had serialized a number of Burroughs' novels, indicated to the author that he wanted only Tarzan tales for the magazines. Nevertheless, on June 26, 1930, Burroughs wrote to Kennicott that he was working on a Western "in an entirely different vein" from his earlier work. "I am in the fourth chapter and so far only one person has been killed. I am trying to make it more ladylike in the hopes of getting it into some . . . publication like *Red Book*." From June 14 to July 12, he wrote the 60,000 word text of the novel, that he called *That Damned Dude*. Despite his hope of achieving a more prestigious publication in a more genteel magazine than usual, Burroughs predicted to Kennicott, "The chances are that I shall not be able to sell it at all." His pessimism was prophetic, for not only Kennicott but the editors of *Elks Magazine, Liberty, The Ladies' Home Journal, Colliers,* and Doubleday Doran rejected it in 1930. In 1931, it was rejected by *The Saturday Eve-*

ning Post and *Argosy*.[1] Munsey's *Argosy* had published much of
Burroughs' earlier work; but the editor, A. H. Bittner, while
admitting that the new novel was "a good, usable regulation
western story," commented that the magazine published few
Westerns and did not welcome any from Burroughs: "Our
readers expect the Tarzan type of story from you and it certainly would disappoint a great many of them to hand them a
western story under your name." Bittner conceded that he
would take a Western only as part of a package, in which it
would follow one of Burroughs' fantastic tales.[2] Accordingly,
Burroughs provided *Argosy* with new Tarzan and Venus novels, but after accepting them, the magazine still rejected *That
Damned Dude*. When the frustrated author suggested publishing it under a "fictitious author's name," the editor responded
that "the story is not for us under any name or at any price. It
is much too conventional and leisurely . . . ."[3] After seven more
years of unproductive negotiations, Burroughs sold it in 1939
to Standard Magazines' *Thrilling Adventures*, where it was
brought out in three installments as "That Damn Dude," "The
Brass Heart," and "The Terrible Tenderfoot" in March, April,
and May, 1939. Retitled *The Deputy Sheriff of Comanche
County*, it was finally brought out in book form in 1940 by the
author's own publishing firm, Edgar Rice Burroughs, Inc.,
which issued all his new novels in hardcover from 1932 on. It
was, in fact, the last book published by the firm for four years
because of the paper shortage during World War II.

The illustrations for the hardcover edition were by John
Coleman Burroughs, the author's third child and second son.
When he was about ten years old, John Coleman started copy-
ing illustrations of his father's work by J. Allen St. John; a few
years later, he began writing adolescent science fiction serials
and illustrating them himself. He graduated magna cum laude
with distinction in art from Pomona College in Claremont, California and was elected to Phi Beta Kappa. In 1936, Edgar Rice
Burroughs dismissed St. John, who had been his favorite illus-
trator, and informed him that thereafter he would have John
Coleman Burroughs illustrate his books. The son illustrated
thirteen of them, beginning with *The Oakdale Affair* (1937) and
The Rider (1937).[4] From 1941 to 1943, he illustrated a Sunday
comic strip of "John Carter of Mars" for United Feature Syn-

dicate. He also illustrated some of Whitman's Big Little Book and Better Little Book versions of some of the Tarzan and Mars books. For Whitman, he collaborated on and probably wrote most of *John Carter and the Giant of Mars* (1940), which first appeared as a Better Little Book before being revised a bit to make up the first half of *John Carter of Mars* (1964), the final volume in the Barsoom series. Later on, John Coleman became a science fiction novelist in his own right with *Treasure of the Black Falcon* (1967).

Burroughs' first three Westerns take place in Arizona in the 1880s and strive for authenticity of time and place. *The Deputy Sheriff of Comanche County* takes place in the 20th century. No date is given, but there are telephones and automobiles and references to Tom Mix movies. Most of the action occurs on a dude ranch rather than a working ranch. Presumably, therefore, the novel was more or less contemporary at the time of composition. It nevertheless retains the code and much of the style of the old West. Automobiles transport visitors between the railroad and the ranch, but thereafter, horses take over. There is a long pursuit sequence in the mountains and desert that requires traditional tracking skills and techniques of desert survival. The hero carves notches on his six-guns, and the action ends in a classic shoot-out. Furthermore, the conflicts between East and West, between culture and self-reliance present similar attitudes and values to those in *The Bandit of Hell's Bend.*

Despite Burroughs' statement that he was trying to make the book "more ladylike," it has all the necessary ingredients to please male Western fans. What Burroughs apparently meant was (as Donald Kennicott complained) that the pace is more leisurely and there is less violence. "I am in the fourth chapter and so far only one person has been killed."[5] By the third chapter of *The Gods of Mars* (1918), on the other hand, John Carter and his Barsoomian comrade-in-arms Tars Tarkas have fought and slaughtered hordes of blood-sucking plant men and 15-foot-high white apes, climbed towering cliffs and explored forbidding caves, fought off innumerable banths and other Martian monsters ("for the better part of an hour one hideous creature after another was launched upon us"), and fought two duels with Martian swordsmen. There is one cliff-hanging episode after another, mostly filled with grotesque horrors as well as violent action. A comparably breathless pace prevails in most of the Tarzan and imaginary world novels.

In *The Deputy Sheriff*, there is very little action until the last third of the book. But there is plenty of episode, and the novel never loses interest. Its more leisurely pace is an advantage in a narrative that depends more upon characterization, which Burroughs' other novels sometimes sacrifice to nonstop action. In *The Deputy Sheriff of Comanche County*, the incidents grow out of character, the interplay of the individuals is more important than in most Burroughs novels, and the style is more restrained. On one level, the story is a murder mystery, which Buck Mason, the deputy sheriff, must solve. His detective work is ingenious enough. But the method of his solving the mystery also makes the novel something of a comedy of manners, as it contrasts Eastern finishing school "culture" with Western pragmatic self-reliance, the Eastern tenderfoot with the Western veteran, and satirizes stereotyped concepts of virility.

Buck Mason, the deputy sheriff of Comanche County, New Mexico, had thought himself in love with Olga Gunderstrom, his childhood sweetheart. She is the daughter of an eccentric and crotchety rancher who rejects Buck as a potential son-in-law, telling him,

"My girl aint fer no low down cowman. Me and her maw was nuthin' but trash . . . . but I made up my mind that my girl was gonna be able to herd with the best of them. That's why I sent her East to school—to keep her away from trash like you and the rest of the slab-sided long-horns that range in Comanche County. My girl ain't gonna know the dirt and sweat and greasy pots in no cowman's kitchen. . . . My girl's gonna marry a swell. . . ."

As it turns out, however, Olga is merely transformed into a snob who becomes ashamed of her Western clothes, manners, and speech. When she returns to the West, she is supercilious, arrogant, and convinced that Buck is a murderer, not because of sufficient evidence but because he lacks refinement, according to her new views.

Buck meanwhile has been educating himself to be worthy of

Olga when she returns. His normal speech is full of nonstandard English—double negatives, "ain't," and the use of "them" as an adjective; he also employs slang and some mild profanity. As Henry Nash Smith points out in *Virgin Land, the American West as Symbol and Myth* (1957), it was a convention in frontier and Western dime novels for the hero and heroine to be aristocrats or at least members of the upper class and to speak perfect academic English. Dialect was a badge of lowly status and disqualified one from being accepted as a lover. As James Fenimore Cooper's Leatherstocking says, when Mabel rejects him in *The Pathfinder* (1826), "I am but a poor hunter, and Mabel, I see, is fit to be an officer's lady." Language is very much a part of this distinction: as Smith observes, "The belief that no one is suitable to conduct a sentimental courtship unless he speaks a pure English is very strong."[6] Accordingly, Buck has been taking correspondence courses in English, reading the classics, studying etiquette, subscribing to *Vogue*, and poring over magazines about golf, polo, and yachting.

At the same time, he worries that his self-education is not "macho"; a real he-man would scorn such things as effeminate. Thus Buck "was ashamed of his library and his reading. He would have hated to have had any of his cronies discover his weakness . . . ." He keeps his books and magazines locked up and considers the book of etiquette and *Vogue* "a reflection upon his manhood." Here Burroughs is ridiculing both sides of the picture. On the one hand, Buck's masculinity can in no way be endangered by his reading or learning standard English. On the other hand, Buck has to a degree accepted Olga's snobbish standards. Just as in *The Bandit of Hell's Bend*, the upper-class heroine finds her cowhand Bull, with his bunkhouse dialect and his indifference to books a more genuine man than the effete Easterners who despise the rough and ready Western life, so Burroughs championed an egalitarian social code. At the same time, as a professional author, he was not about to deride literacy or scoff at culture. It is the pretentious snobbery of those with a cultural veneer on the one hand and anti-intellectualism parading as masculinity on the other that he derided.

Accused of the murder of Gunderstrom, Buck submits himself to further mental agonies when he disguises himself as Bruce Marvel, a wealthy Eastern aristocrat, and turns up at a dude ranch dressed in the latest English polo costume. The cowboys sneer at him and indulge in "flippant remarks" at "his sartorial effulgence." They fear that he'll get his "panties" dirty, "And then what'll your mama say?" At the end, when his true identity is revealed, he confesses, "I really felt worse about them funny pants and the boot garters than I did about being accused of killin' a man; for I knew that I could clear myself from the latter in court, but I might never live down the other." Though the men who ridicule him are criminals, far less skilled than Buck at riding and gunplay, he has not been able to outgrow their attitudes and the prejudices of Western provincialism.

It is, of course, a convention in swashbuckling fiction and films to have the dashing hero pretend to be an effeminate fop. Much of the fun of the movies *The Mark of Zorro* (1920, remade in 1940), Baroness Orczy's *The Scarlet Pimpernel* (1934), and *The Son of Monte Cristo* (1940) comes from this deception, for the readers or audience know that the seeming sissy is actually the most virile person around. Thus Buck (or Bruce) pretends to know nothing about horses, requests an English saddle and an exceedingly gentle beast, and has the ranch manager top his mount for him each morning. He patterns his riding technique after that of fat Mrs. Talbot Birdie, prompting one of the cowhands to say, ". . . it gives me a pain to see anything that calls itself a man ride like that." In a shooting exhibition, he misses the mark altogether. He employs the bookish language of his correspondence course English and addresses the ranch hands as "my man."

Despite his appreciation of authentic culture, Burroughs repeatedly criticized urban civilization and expressed a preference for a rugged outdoor life. Lord Greystoke always feels a renewal of freedom when he strips off his clothes, sloughs off the "veneer" of civilation, and once more becomes Tarzan, lord of the jungle. Likewise, in *The Deputy Sheriff of Comanche County*, Burroughs condemns "the males of the third generation, educated at Eastern colleges, softened by contact with the luxuries of large cities" who had let the TF Ranch in Portoco County, Arizona deteriorate into a dude ranch. (Though Comanche County is in New Mexico, most of the book takes place, like Burroughs' other Westerns, in Arizona.)

Despite his supposed love for Olga, Buck finds himself reluctantly attracted to Kay White, a California visitor to the dude ranch. Unlike the other guests, who dress in a variety of outlandish attire, like characters "out of the latest Western movie thriller," Kay looks natural in denim overalls and workshirt. Though she is from a wealthy family, she is no snob. When the others ridicule Marvel, she is tolerant and understanding, whereas another guest who "three weeks previously, had never been west of Philadelphia" derides Marvel as a tenderfoot. As Marvel, Bruce is seemingly more inept than effeminate; in banter with the men, he gives better than he gets, and when Kay's horse, frightened by gunfire, runs away with her, it is Marvel who rides like a centaur to her rescue. At times, he cannot help dropping the mask; when off guard, he slips up on grammar and relapses into double negatives. Kay comes to believe he is a nouveau riche Westerner pretending to be an Eastern aristocrat. She herself is without pretenses. She prefers practical clothes to artificial attire and takes people as they are. When Cory Blaine, the ranch manager, complains to her that he is "an ignorant cuss" who lacks book learning, she says, "There is a lot of knowledge in the world that is not in any book. Some of the most ignorant people in the world are scholars. . . . It takes something more than a knowledge of English to constitute a gentleman. . . ." She also admits that if she loved a man, she would marry him no matter what his background or social standing. At the end, the deputy sheriff drops his academic English altogether and falls back into his natural dialect, but Kay accepts him anyhow.

The treatment of love is both subtle and restrained. Kay "conceived of love as a devastating passion, compelling and unreasoning; and certainly no man had ever aroused such an emotion in her breast; but she realized that she might be mistaken." She resists Blaine's crude but impassioned wooing. Kay is not a snob, but she has the good sense to realize that few marriages between wealthy girls and their stable managers or chauffeurs turn out happily,

not because of the positions that the men held, but because everything
in their training and environment and in the training and environment of their friends had been so different from that to which the girls
had been accustomed that neither could find comfort nor happiness
in the social sphere of the other.

On the other hand, she finds herself attracted to Bruce in spite
of herself. He is equally attracted but tries to resist because of
his loyalty to Olga. There is a fair amount of discussion as to
what draws people together and what constitutes a sound ba-
sis for marriage. Kay thinks that all too often people marry on
the crest of a wave of unreasoning instinct when they have
nothing else in common. She and Bruce, on the other hand, fall
in love gradually and reluctantly. Kay finds his society a relief;

Marvel was companionable in that he was silent when she did not
wish to talk; or equally willing to uphold his end of the conversation
when she felt in the mood for it. . . . It spoke well for the companionship of both of them that no matter how long these silences they never
became strained. . . .

Despite his pretended foppishness on the one hand and his relapses into ungrammatical crudities and social faux pas on the
other, Bruce has a natural dignity, a sense of reliability that
appeals to her.

Bruce finally proves himself a hero in the last third of the
book, when Burroughs falls back upon one of his favorite plot
devices—having the heroine abducted and rescued after a long
and arduous search by the hero. This part of the novel is re-
deemed from standard melodramatics by Burroughs' detailed
knowledge of Western terrain and the techniques of tracking
and survival in mountains and desert. The pursuit sequence
also shows Burroughs' skill at horsemanship, for the villain is
a rider but not a horseman, with no consideration for his
mount, whereas Bruce succeeds in catching up with the abductors and then taking Kay out of the waterless desert by his
knowledge both of the country and of his horse. His self-confidence impresses her, though she is shocked by the seeming casualness with which he kills one of her abductors.

The concluding love scene is handled with subtle indirec-
tion. Whereas Tarzan "took his woman in his arms and smoth-

ered her upturned, panting lips with kisses," so that Jane's "Hot, sweet breath against his cheek and mouth had fanned a new flame to life within his breast, and perfect lips had clung to his in burning kisses that seared a deep brand into his soul," *The Deputy Sheriff of Comanche County* ends with Kay's friend Dora observing a distant figure "standing among the cottonwoods by the river; and when she looked more closely and saw that the one figure was really two, she smiled and turned her eyes in another direction."

Burroughs no doubt enjoyed having his stalwart hero disguised as a tenderfoot who is really a better horseman and marksman than anyone because he himself had twice been treated as a tenderfoot, only to turn the tables on his scoffers. When his father sent him, at age 15, to an Idaho cattle ranch in 1891, the local ranchers, cowboys, and miners with whom he came into contact considered him a comical greenhorn, but he learned fast and passed the various tests of initiation and manhood. Although his only previous riding had been on ponies in a city park, he quickly became an expert horseman who often rode 60 miles round trip in a day carrying mail from the ranch to American Fork. On one occasion, when instructed to ride out to the pasture and bring back some horses to the corrals, he mounted an unfamiliar horse that was already saddled and bridled instead of saddling up one of the ranch horses. Burroughs did not know that this was a notoriously cantankerous beast that had been brought to the ranch by a celebrated bronco-buster. The tenderfoot failed to check the cinch, which was loose; and as horse and rider climbed up a bank of the Raft River, the saddle slipped off over the horse's hindquarters and Burroughs tumbled into the dirt behind the four-legged terror. "He should have killed me, but instead he stopped with the cinch around his hind feet and turned an inquiring glance back at me." Burroughs saddled him up again and brought in the rounded-up horses. When he returned "safe and alive, on the worst horse in Cassia County," his brothers and the ranch hands stared at him "goggle-eyed."[7]

Burroughs also succeeded in taming a horse named Whisky Jack, who "had killed one man and mained several others." On his first attempt, the horse slipped and fell on top of Burroughs, who was so game to try him again that his owner, Jim

Pierce, a local cattle king, offered to given him Whisky Jack if he could ride him. The first time he tried, the ranch hands had to throw and hogtie the horse before they could get a saddle and bridle on him, but Burroughs persisted: "I stayed on him all that day because I was afraid if I got off I could never get on again." Eventually he tamed the horse, though the first time he put the mail bags on Whisky Jack, the animal "ran for ten miles before he became resigned to the fact that he couldn't leave the mail bags behind."[8] In time, Burroughs became a consummately skilled rider as well as a lover of horses: "When I got my leg over a horse," he stated, "I owned the world."[9]

Back in school at the Michigan Military Academy, he further improved his horsemanship and won second prize at a Columbian Saddle Horse Show sponsored by the Detroit Riding Club in April, 1893. He recalled that at the Academy, "We did a great deal of trick riding in those days—bareback, Cossack, Graeco-Roman, and all the rest of it."[10] Upon graduation, he joined the Army and was sent to the Seventh Cavalry at Fort Grant, Arizona, in 1896. When he was assigned to lessons in horsemanship, his instructor told the sergeant a few days later, "Why in hell did you send me that bird? He can ride better than I can."[11] Burroughs' niece, Mrs. Evelyn McKenzie, with whose family he lived for a while in Idaho, recalled that "he rode magnificently, as much one with the horse as an Indian."[12]

Thus Burroughs himself quickly changed from tenderfoot to veteran and amused himself by having Buck Mason seemingly go the other route in his transformation to Bruce Marvel.

Why did Burroughs write no more Westerns after *The Deputy Sheriff of Comanche County?* With his endlessly fertile gift of storytelling, it is unlikely that he had run out of ideas. But his Westerns did not fit into any of his ongoing series, and it was not only easier to turn out another Tarzan, Mars, Venus, or Pellucidar novel than to create a self-contained Western, but the former is what his readers had come to expect and to demand. As he wrote to Sir Algernon Methuen before beginning his first Western, he feared the book "might have little or no value here, since the readers . . . seem to prefer my highly imaginative stuff."[13] Though they are eminently cinematic, none were picked up by the movies, despite the popularity of

Tarzan films. During the 1930s, in fact, Hollywood filmed very
few big budget Westerns; between 1931 and 1939, only four
Westerns *(The Plainsman* [1936], *Wells Fargo* [1937], *The Texas
Rangers* [1936], and *The Texans* [1938])￼ were produced by major studios; otherwise, the Western degenerated during the
decade into B-class productions or serials, until the genre was
revived in 1939 with *Dodge City* (1939), *Union Pacific* (1939),
Destry Rides Again (1939), *Jesse James* (1939), and *Stagecoach*
(1939). Thus there was little incentive for Burroughs to continue creating Westerns, and the frustrating experience of his
nine years' delay in publishing *The Deputy Sheriff of Comanche
County* undoubtedly discouraged him from further efforts in
this direction. It is a pity, for although only four of his seventy
or so novels, plus sections of a few others (*A Princess of Mars*
[1917], *The Mucker* [1921], *The Girl from Hollywood* [1923], and
The Moon Men [1926]) deal with the West, those four contain
some of his most solid work. Though Burroughs' total contri-
bution to the Western is not extensive, it is notable, and with
more encouragement, he might have become a major writer of
popular Westerns.

Robert E. Morsberger
California State Polytechnic University
Pomona, California

REFERENCES

1. Irwin Porges, *Edgar Rice Burroughs, the Man Who Created Tarzan* (Provo, Utah: Brigham Young University Press, 1975), pp. 525, 760.

2. Porges, p. 525.

3. Porges, p. 526.

4. Porges, pp. 437, 575.

5. Edgar Rice Burroughs to Donald Kennicott, June 26, 1930.

6. Henry Nash Smith, *Virgin Land, The American West as Symbol and Myth* (New York: Random House Vintage Books, 1957), p. 108.

7. Porges, p. 21.

8. Edgar Rice Burroughs, Letter to Conroy Gillespie, May 17, 1935.

9. Porges, p. 21.

10. Edgar Rice Burroughs, unpublished *Autobiography*, 1929.

11. Edgar Rice Burroughs, letter to Hugh Thomason, November 20, 1929.

12. Robert W. Fenton, *The Big Swingers* (Englewood Cliffs, New Jersey: Prentice-Hall, 1967), p. 29.

13. Porges, p. 400.

Pitched forward upon his face

TO

Mary Lucas Pflueger

CONTENTS

7

8 CONTENTS

THE DEPUTY SHERIFF OF COMANCHE COUNTY

i

THE LINE FENCE

A LONE rider drew rein before a gate consisting of three poles cut from straight pine saplings. He leaned from the saddle and dropped one end of each of the two upper bars to the ground, stepped his horse over the remaining bar and, stooping again, replaced the others. Then he rode slowly along a dirt road that showed little signs of travel.

As he rode he seemed but an animated part of the surrounding landscape, so perfectly did he harmonize from the crown of his Stetson to the light shod hoofs of his pony.

Everything that he wore seemed a part of him, as he seemed a part of his horse. His well worn chaps, his cartridge belt and holster, his shirt and bandana, like the leather of his horse trappings, were toned and mellowed by age and usage; yet they carried the same suggestion of strength and freshness and efficiency as did his bronzed face and his clear, gray eyes.

His mount moved at an easy, shuffling gait that some horsemen might call a rack, but which the young man would have described as a pace.

The horse was that homeliest of all horse colors, a blue roan, the only point of distinction in his appearance being a circular white spot, about the size of a saucer, that encircled his right eye, a marking which could not be said to greatly enhance his beauty, though it had served another and excellent purpose in suggesting his name — Bull's Eye.

At first glance the young man might have been found as little remarkable as his horse. In New Mexico there are probably thousands of other young men who look very much like him. His one personal adornment, in which he took a quiet, secret pride, was a flowing, brown mustache with drooping ends, which accomplished little more than to collect alkali dust and hide an otherwise strong and handsome mouth, while the low drawn brim of his Stetson almost accomplished the same result for the man's finest features — a pair of unusually arresting gray eyes.

The road wound through low rolling hills covered with stunted cedars, beyond which rose a range of mountains, whose sides were clothed with pine, the dark green of which was broken occasionally by irregular patches of quaking aspens, the whole mellowed and softened and mysterized by an enveloping purple haze.

The road, whose parallel twin paths suggested wheels of traffic, but in whose dust appeared only the spoor of hoofed animals, wound around the shoulder of a hill and debouched into a small valley, in the center of which stood a dilapidated log house.

"This here," said the young man to his pony, "is where we were headed fer. I hope the old man's in," and as though to assure him of the fulfillment of his wish, the door of the cabin opened and a large, droop-shouldered, gray haired man emerged.

"Ev'nen, Ole," said the rider.

"Ev'nen," said the older man, rather shortly, as the other stopped his horse and swung from the saddle. "What you doin' here?"

"I come to see you about that line fence, Ole," said the young man.

"Gol durned if you aint as bad as your pa," said the older man. "I aint heared nuthin' else but that durned line fence fer the last twenty years."

"You and the old man fit over that fence for eighteen years up to the very day he died, but I'll be doggoned if I want to scrap about it."

"Then what you doin' up here about it?" demanded the other.

"I aint up here to scrap with you, Ole. I just come up to tell you."

"Tell me what?"

"You aint doin' nuthin' with that land. You aint never done nuthin' with it. You can't get water on to it. I can and there's about a hundred acres of it that lies right for alfalfa and joins right on to the patch I put in last year."

"Well what you goin' to do about it?   It's my land.   You sure can't put alfalfa on my land."

"It aint your land, Ole, and you know it.   You put your line fence in the wrong place.   May be you did it accidental at first, but you know well enough that you aint got no title to that land."

"Well I got it fenced and I have had it fenced for twenty years.   That's title enough for me," growled Gunderstrom.

"Now listen, Ole; I said I didn't come up here figurin' on quarrelin' with you and I aint a goin' to.   I'm just tellin' you, I'm goin' to move that fence and put in alfalfa."

Olaf Gunderstrom's voice trembled with suppressed anger as he replied.   "If ye lay a hand on that fence of mine, Buck Mason, I'll kill you."

"Now don't make me quarrel with you, Ole," said the young man, "cause I don't want to do nuthin' like that.   I'm gonna move the fence, and I'm gonna say here that if anybody gets shot, it aint me.   Now let's don't chaw any more fat over that.   What do you hear from Olga?"

"None of your durn business," snapped Gunderstrom.

Mason grinned.   "Well, Ogla and I grew up

together as kids," he reminded the older man, "and I'm just naturally interested in her."

"Well, I'll thank you to mind your own business, Buck Mason," said Gunderstrom surlily. "My girl aint fer no low down cowman. Me and her maw was nuthin' but trash. We seen it once when we went to Frisco and I aint never been nowhere since, but I made up my mind that my girl was gonna be able to herd with the best of 'em. That's why I sent her East to school — to keep her away from trash like you and the rest of the slab-sided longhorns that range in Comanche County.

"My girl aint gonna know the dirt and sweat and greasy pots in no cowman's kitchen. She aint gonna have no swells high hattin' her. She's goin' to be in a position to do the high hattin' herself. God and her mother give her the looks; the schools back in the states can give her the education, and I can give her the money; so she can herd with the best of 'em. My girl's gonna marry a swell; so you needn't waste your time asking no more questions about her. You aint never goin' to see her again, and if you do she won't even know you."

"Come, come, Ole," said Mason, "don't get so excited. I wasn't aimin' on bitin' Olga. She was a good kid; and we used to have a lot of fun together; and, say, if Olga marries a duke she wouldn't never high hat none of her old friends."

"She won't never get a chance while I'm alive," said Gunderstrom. "She aint never comin' back here."

"That's your business and hers," said Mason. "It aint none o'mine." He swung easily into the saddle. "I'll be moseyin' along, Ole. So long!"

"Listen," cried the older man as Mason wheeled his horse to move away. "Remember what I said about that line fence. If you lay a hand on it I'll kill you."

Buck Mason reined in his pony and turned in his saddle. "I hope there aint nobody goin' to be killed, Ole," he said quietly; "but if there is it aint goin' to be me. Come on, Bull's Eye, it's a long way back to town."

But Buck Mason did not ride to town. Instead he stopped at his own lonely ranch house, cooked his supper and afterward sat beneath an oil lamp and read.

The book that he was reading he had taken

from a cupboard, the door of which was secured
by a padlock, for the sad truth was that Mason
was ashamed of his library and of his reading.
He would have hated to have had any of his
cronies discover his weakness, for the things that
he read were not of the cow country. They in-
cluded a correspondence course in English, a
number of the classics which the course had
recommended, magazines devoted to golf, polo,
yachting, and a voluminous book on etiquette;
but perhaps the thing that caused him the greatest mental perturbation in anticipation of its discovery by his candid, joke-loving friends was a
file of the magazine *Vogue*.

No one knew that Buck Mason pored over
these books and magazines whenever he had a
leisure moment; in fact, no one suspected that he
possessed them; and he would have died rather
than to have explained why he did so.

He had led rather a lonely life, even before his
father had died two years previously; but perhaps the greatest blow he had ever suffered had
been the departure of Olga Gunderstrom for the
East, nearly six years before.

She was sixteen then, and he eighteen. They

had never spoken of love; perhaps neither one of them had thought of love; but she was the only girl that he had ever known well. When she had gone and he had commenced to realize how much he missed her, and then gradually to understand the barrier that her education was destined to raise between them, he began to believe that he loved her and that life without her would be a drab and monotonous waste.

Perhaps it was because he was a little bashful with women and guessed that he would never be well enough acquainted with any other girl to ask her to be his wife. He knew that he and Olga would get along well together. He knew that he would always be happy with her, and he thought that this belief constituted love; so he determined to fit himself as best he might to appear well in the society that he believed her superior education destined her to enter, that she might not ever have cause to be ashamed of him.

It was a pathetic little weakness. He did not think of it as pathetic but only as a weakness, and he was very much ashamed of it. Like most quiet men, he had a horror of ridicule; and so he always kept his books and his magazines locked in his cupboard, nor ever took one out unless he was alone, except that when he took one of those long, lonely trips, which were sometimes made necessary in pursuance of his office as deputy sheriff of Comanche County, he would carry one of his books along with him; but never the book of etiquette or a copy of *Vogue,* each of which he considered a reflection upon his manhood.

In another lonely cabin, several miles away, Olaf Gunderstrom had cooked his own frugal meal, washed his dishes and gone to bed.

He was an eccentric old man, and he had permitted his eccentricities to become more and more marked after the death of his wife and the departure of his daughter for the East.

Possibly the wealthiest man in the county, he lived in the meanest of cabins, notwithstanding the fact that he had a comfortable, if not luxurious home in the county seat; and always he lived alone. His ranch and cow hands had their headquarters on another one of his ranches, several miles from Gunderstrom's shack. He rode there every day, and sometimes he ate dinner with them; but he always returned to his lonely cabin for his supper.

His only pleasures in life were directing his business, computing his profits and dreaming of the future of his daughter; and, before he fell asleep this night, his mind thus occupied with his daughter, he was reminded of the visit of Buck Mason in the afternoon.

"Always a askin' about Olga," he soliloquized grumblingly. "Never see that fellah that he aint askin' me about Olga. Guess he thinks I can't see right through him like a ladder. He'd like to marry Ole Gunderstrom's daughter. That's what he'd like to do and get his paws on all my land and cattle; but he aint aggona get Olga, and he aint even goin' to get that quarter section. I've had a fence around that for more'n twenty years now; and I guess if that don't give me no title, nuthin' else does. Buck Mason! Huh!" he snorted in disgust, and with Mason still in his thoughts he fell asleep.

ii

WHO KILLED GUNDERSTROM?

THE NIGHT wore on, its silence broken once by the hoot of an owl and again by the distant yapping of a coyote; and Olaf Gunderstrom slept.

Toward midnight subdued sounds floated up from the twin trails that wound in from the highway — the mellowed creaking of old leather, mingled with the breathing of horses — and then darker shadows moved beneath the moonless sky, slowly taking form and shape until they became distinguishable as five horsemen.

In silence they rode to the shack and dismounted where a long tie rail paralleled the front of the building. They moved very softly, making no noise in dismounting, nor speaking any words. They tied their horses to the tie rail and approached the door of the cabin. To the mystery of their silent approach there was added a sinister note by the handkerchiefs tied across their faces just below their eyes. Men come not thus at night in friendliness or well meaning.

Gently the leader pushed open the door, which was as innocent of bar and lock as are most cabin doors behind which no woman dwells.

Silently the five entered the single room of the cabin. The leader approached the wooden cot, roughly built against one of the cabin walls, where Gunderstrom lay asleep. It was dark within the cabin, but not so dark but that one familiar with the interior could locate the cot and the form of the sleeper. In the hand of the man crossing the room so stealthily was a long-barreled Colt.

The silent intruder could see the cot and the outlines of the blur that was the sleeper upon it; but he did not see one of Gunderstrom's boots that lay directly in his path, and he stepped partially upon it and half stumbled and as he did so, Gunderstrom awoke and sat up. "Buck Mason!" he exclaimed. "What do you want here?" and at the same time he reached for the gun that lay always beside him.

There was a flash in the dark, the silence was split by the report of a pistol and Olaf Gunderstrom slumped back upon his blanket, a bullet in his brain.

For a few moments the killer stood above his prey, seeking perhaps to assure himself that his work has been well done. He did not move, nor did his companions, nor did the dead man upon the cot. Presently the killer leaned low and placed his ear upon the breast of Gunderstrom. When he straightened up he turned back toward the doorway.

"We'd better be on our way," he said, and as the five men filed out of the cabin and mounted their horses, no other words were spoken. As silently as they had come they disappeared along the twin trails that led down to the highway.

*   *   *   *   *

It was nine o'clock in the morning. The sheriff of Comanche County sat in his office. He had read his mail and was now immersed in a newspaper.

An old man, leaning in the doorway, spit dexterously across the wooden porch into the dust of the road and shifted his quid. He, too, was reading a newspaper.

"Seems mighty strange to me," he said, "that nobody aint caught these fellers yet."

"There don't nobody know who they be," said the sheriff.

"I see by the papers," said the old man, "that they think they got a line on 'em."

"They aint got nuthin' on 'em," snapped the sheriff. "They don't even know that it's the same gang."

"No, that's right," assented the old man, "but it sure does look suspicious. Robbin' and murderin' and rustlin' breakin' out all of a sudden in towns here where we aint had none o' it for years. Why say, in the last year there's been more Hell goin' on around in this neck of the woods and over into Arizony than I've saw all put together for ten year before."

At this juncture the telephone bell rang and the sheriff rose and walked to the instrument, where it hung against the wall.

"Hello," he said as he put the receiver to his ear, and then, "The hell you say!" He listened for a moment longer. "Don't touch nuthin' — leave everything as it is. I'll notify the Coroner and then I'll be out as soon as I can."

He hung up the receiver and as he turned away from the instrument Buck Mason entered the office. "Mornin', sheriff!" he said.

"Good morning, Buck!" returned the sheriff.

"Who's killed now?" demanded old man Cage, who, having heard half the conversation and scenting excitement, had abandoned his post in the doorway and entered the room.

Buck Mason looked inquiringly at the sheriff. "Somebody killed?" he asked.

The sheriff nodded. "Tom Kidder just called me up from the Circle G home ranch. He says they found old man Gunderstrom shot to death in his shack over on Spring Creek."

"Gunderstrom?" he exclaimed. "Why I see —," he hesitated. "Do they know who done it?" The sheriff shook his head. "Perhaps I better get right over there," continued Mason.

"I wish you would, Buck," said the sheriff. "Got your horse?"

"Yes."

"I got to pick up Doc Bellows; and you can be there, if you cut across the hills, long before I can shag Lizzie around by the roads."

"I'll be gettin' along then," said Mason, and as he left the office and mounted his horse the sheriff strapped on his gun and prepared to go after the coroner.

"Looks to me like that hit Buck pretty hard," said old man Cage. "Warnt he kinda soft on that Gunderstrom heifer?"

Bull's Eye carried his master at an easy lope across the flat toward the hills, where there was a stiff and rocky climb to the summit and an equally precipitous drop into Spring Valley, where Gunderstrom's shack lay a scant five miles from town by trail.

Uncle Billy Cage had resumed his position in the doorway of the office as the sheriff departed to look for the coroner. Half way to his car, the officer stopped and turned back. "If you aint got nuthin' else to do, sorta hang around the office until I get back, Uncle Billy. Will you?" he asked.

"I'll stay here as long as I can, sheriff," replied the old man. "May be I better go and fetch my bed."

"Shucks. I won't be gone long," the sheriff assured him.

"I don't know about that," replied Cage. "It's twenty mile of rough road from here to Gunderstrom's shack, and Lizzie aint what she used to be."

"Shucks. I could take her over the horse trail, Uncle Billy, if I wasn't afraid of scaring Doc Bellows," replied the sheriff with a grin.

As Buck Mason rode up to the Gunderstrom shack he was greeted by Tom Kidder, foreman of the Circle G outfit, and two of the cowhands. The three men were squatting on their heels in the shade of a tree near the shack; and as Mason approached, Kidder rose. "Hello, Buck!" he said.

"Hello, Tom!" replied Mason. "How's everything?"

"Oh, so so," replied the foreman. "I reckon the sheriff told you."

"Yeah, that's why I'm here. You fellers aint been messin' around here none, have you?"

"No," replied Kidder. "When the old man didn't show up at the home ranch this morning, I rode over. I went in the shack, and when I seen there wasn't nuthin' to be done for him I rode back to the ranch and called up the sheriff. There aint been nobody in the shack since."

"Got any idea who done it?" asked Mason.

"No," replied the foreman. "There's been horses in and out from the highway recently. You could see that plain in the dirt; and there were horses tied up to his hitchin' rail last night, but I didn't mess around here any after what the sheriff told me. So everything's about like it was after the old man croaked."

"I'll take a look around," said Mason, who had dismounted.

Dropping his reins to the ground, he approached the shack. He moved slowly and deliberately, his keen eyes searching for any sign that the soft earth might give back to him. For several minutes he scrutinized the ground about the hitching rail, and then he entered the shack.

Inside he disturbed nothing, but examined

everything minutely. For a brief moment he paused at the side of the cot, looking down into the upturned face of the dead man, the ghastliness of which was accentuated by the wound in the center of the pallid forehead.

Whatever thoughts the sight engendered in the mind of Buck Mason were not reflected in his calm, inscrutable gaze.

At Mason's feet lay the boot upon which the murderer had stepped and stumbled; and to it the eyes of the deputy dropped, casually at first and then with aroused interest. He stooped down then and examined it closely, but he did not touch it. After a moment he straightened up and left the shack, pausing again to make another examination of the ground about the hitching rail.

As he joined the men beneath the tree they looked at him inquiringly. "Well," asked Kidder, "what do you make of it?"

Mason squatted down upon his heels, his eyes upon the ground. "Well," he said, "there were five of them. At least there were five horses tied to the hitching rail last night, and that's about all we have to go on."

"About all? What do you mean?"

"There aint much more except that it don't look like a case of robbery. As far as I can see there wasn't nuthin' touched in the shack."

"A lot of folks thought the old man kept money hidden here," said Kidder.

"Yes, I know that," replied Mason, "and I expected to find the shack all torn to pieces where they searched for it."

"Mebbe he give it to 'em," suggested one of the cowhands.

"I reckon you didn't know old man Gunderstrom very well then," said the foreman. "In the first place he never kept no money here, and in the second place he wouldn't have told them where it was if he had."

"I think he had started to reach for his gun," said Mason.

"Mebbe that's why they bored him," suggested the cowhand.

"Maybe," assented Mason.

"This'll be tough on the girl," said Kidder.

Mason made no comment. His eyes were searching the ground all about the three men, though they did not know it.

"I reckon she'll live through it," said the cow-hand, "especially after she gets a slant at her bank balance. She'll be the richest gal in a dozen counties."

"There'll be plenty hombres campin' on her trail now," said the foreman, shooting a quick, shrewd glance at Mason.

"Did the old man have any squabbles with any-body lately?" asked the deputy sheriff.

"He was a hard man to do business with," replied Kidder; "and there's lots of folks around here that didn't have much use for him, but there aint no one that I know of that had any call to kill him."

"Did he have any new business deals on with anyone that you know of?"

"I didn't know nuthin' about his business," replied Kidder; "he kept that to himself. But I've seen signs around the shack before that there'd been fellers up here at night. I don't know who they was or what they come for, and I never seen 'em. I just seen horse tracks around once in a while; and I knew fellers had been here, but it was none of my business, and I kept my mouth shut."

"Here comes a car," said the cowhand.

"That'll be the sheriff and the coroner," said Mason.

"Lizzie made pretty good time," said Kidder. "They must have packed her on their shoulders and run."

"She's hittin' on two and a half," said the cowhand; "which is better than I ever seen her do before."

As the car wheezed to a stop, the fat and jovial Doc Bellows lowered himself ponderously to the ground; and after the brief greetings of the cow country he asked a few questions.

"When you go in the shack," said Mason, "I wish you'd both notice that boot of Ole's that's lying in front of the cot. You seen it, didn't you, Kidder?" The foreman nooded. "Well," continued Mason, "guess all of you'll remember where you seen it; and then, sheriff, I wish you'd take care of it and not let nobody touch it."

"Is that a clue?" demanded the sheriff.

"I don't know that it amounts to nuthin'" replied Mason, "but I'd like to have the chance to follow it up."

"Sure," said the sheriff.

"All right then, I'll be gettin' along," replied the deputy. "There aint nuthin' more I can do here," and as the other men entered the shack he mounted and turned Bull's Eye's nose down the road toward the main highway.

It was late when the sheriff returned to his office, but Uncle Billy Cage was still there.

"There weren't no call for you to stay all night, Uncle Billy," said the sheriff.

"I wanted to see you," said the old man. "I got some important news for you, but by gum I don't believe it."

"What is it?" demanded the sheriff.

"About an hour after you left the telephone rung and some feller at the other end that talked like he had a harelip said, 'Is this the sheriff's office?' and I said, 'Yes'; and he said, 'Do you want to know who killed Gunderstrom?' and I said, 'Sure'; and he said, 'Well, it was Buck Mason,' and then he hung up."

"I don't believe it," said the sheriff.

"Neither do I," said Uncle Billy Cage.

iii

BRUCE MARVEL

THE TF RANCH in Porico County, Arizona, had fallen upon bad days. For three generations its great ranges, its wooded mountains, its widely scattered streams and water holes had remained in one family; but the males of the third generation, educated at Eastern colleges, softened by contact with the luxuries of large cities, had left their vast principality in the hands of salaried managers and contemporaneously the cattle business had suffered one of its periodic slumps.

33

It is not necessary to go into the harrowing details that are all too familiar to cattle men. Several years before, title had passed to a group of banks that held paper far in excess of the present value of the property, which, in order to maintain grazing rights on Government land, had been forced into the operation of the ranch while they sought frantically and futilely for a buyer all the way from the Atlantic to the Pacific.

An experienced cattle man was operating the business for them in an endeavor to make expenses; and following his policy of taking advantage of every opportunity to augment the income, he had leased the home ranch together with the hunting and fishing privileges of the entire property to Cory Blaine, who had thus become a pioneer in the dude ranch business.

It takes time and capital to establish a going business, and Cory Blaine had discovered that a dude ranch was no exception to the rule.

For two years it had been rather hard sledding, but at last he felt that the venture was on the high road to success. The number of his guests was satisfactory and so were their bank accounts, but even so Cory Blaine was not perfectly satisfied.

He wanted more than a living.   He wanted big money; and the more he came in contact with people who had it, the more determined he had become to have it himself; for Cory Blaine's ambition was developed almost to the point of a disease.

He was sitting late one afternoon upon the front porch of the ranch house with some of his guests when a buckboard swung into sight on the dusty road that wound for miles through the property down to the railroad.

"Here comes the tenderfoot," said a man from Boston, who, three weeks previously, had never been west of Philadelphia.

"I hope he can play bridge," said a fat lady in khaki bloomers and high heeled shoes.

"I'm just hoping he can stay on a horse without help," said Blaine.

The buckboard that was approaching, drawn by a team of bronchos, was the result of Cory Blaine's instinct for showmanship.   He used it exclusively to transport his guests between the railroad and the ranch house, feeling that it lent an atmosphere that no automobile could induce.

The man who drove the buckboard was also a

showman, as was evidenced by the magnificent style in which he drew up in front of the ranch house, covering the last two or three hundred yards at a gallop, setting the bronchos on their haunches in a cloud of dust at the finish.

A couple of cowhands had sauntered over from the bunk house when the buckboard had first appeared in the distance; and as Bruce Marvel alighted, they were unroping his trunk at the back of the vehicle while they sized him up with inward contempt. All other eyes were upon the new arrival as Cory Blaine descended from the porch and took him by the hand.

"You'd be Mr. Marvel, I reckon," said Blaine.

"Yes," replied the newcomer.

"My name's Blaine," said the host. "I'm glad to meet you."

"Thanks," said Marvel.

"Have a good trip?"

"Yes, but a dirty one. I'd like to go to my room and clean up."

"Sure," said Blaine. "Come ahead. The boys will be right up with your stuff," and he led the way into the house, followed by his new guest.

"Here ye are," said Blaine, opening the door

of a small box-like room. "Guess you'll find everything here you need. When yer done come on
out and meet the rest of the folks. We feed at
six o'clock. It's pretty near that now."

"By the way," said Marvel as Blaine was leaving, "shall I dress for dinner?"

"Aint you dressed now?" asked the other.

"I mean do the men wear dinner clothes? —
tuxedos, you know."

Blaine tried to hide the pity in his heart as he
explained that that was not at all necessary; but
when he closed the door behind him he grinned;
and upon the other side of the door his guest
grinned, too.

"What do you suppose?" asked Blaine as he
joined the others on the porch.

"What?" asked a girl in overalls.

"He wants to know if he should put on a spike
tailed coat and a stove pipe hat for dinner."

"My God!" exclaimed a young woman, who
was rigged up in an outfit that would have turned
Tom Mix green with envy. "He's got a lot to
learn."

"Perhaps," said the blond girl in overalls, "he
is just trying to be himself and act natural. You

know there are a lot of people who dress for dinner every night."

"When you are in Rome, do as the Romans do," said the man from Boston.

"Give him a chance," said the blond girl, "and don't forget that on the first camping trip we took after you arrived you brought along green silk pajamas."

"Oh, come now, Kay," he expostulated. "That's different."

"Did you notice his luggage?" said the Tom Mix girl. "Brand new and his clothes, too. He must have bought a whole new outfit just to rough it in."

"I hope he can play bridge," said the fat lady.

"I'll bet he plays ping-pong," said Bert Adams, the man from Boston.

"I think he is real nice looking," interjected Miss Pruell, Kay White's spinster aunt.

Twenty minutes later silence fell upon the company as Marvel came out onto the porch — one of those uncomfortable silences that may last but a moment and still seem endless.

This one Cory Blaine relieved by introducing Marvel to his other guests, and a moment later

the clatter of an iron pipe on a metal triangle announced the evening meal.

At the long table Bruce Marvel found himself
seated between Kay White, the blond in overalls,
and Dora Crowell, the Tom Mix girl.

He had noticed the difference in the apparel of
the two girls; and though he was duly impressed
by the ornate trappings of Dora, he thought that
the other girl somehow looked more genuine in
her blue overalls pulled over high heeled boots,
her denim workshirt, and a bandanna handkerchief knotted loosely about her throat. He surmised that she belonged here and this supposition
prompted his first question.

"This is your home, Miss White?" he asked.

"It commences to look like it," she replied. "I
have been here two months now, but my real
home is in California."

"What time do we start tomorrow, Cory?"
asked Adams.

"Almost any time you folks want to," replied
Blaine. "The chuck wagon went on ahead today
as far as Mill Creek. That's only about fifteen
miles. I didn't want to make it too hard the first
day."

"We're going on a lion hunt," Kay White explained to Marvel. "We had planned on leaving yesterday, but when Cory got your telegram he decided to wait so that you could go along with us."

"Can you ride?" demanded Dora Crowell.

"I guess I can manage," replied Marvel, "but I suppose these cow horses aren't much like polo ponies."

"Do you play bridge, Mr. Marvel?" demanded Mrs. Talbot.

"Do you play bridge here?" he asked.

"I can't get any one to play with me," complained the fat lady. "Those that play say they get enough of it at home."

"Well I suppose that's true," agreed Marvel. "What we want here is a change."

"Then I suppose you won't play with me either," whined Mrs. Talbot.

"We might get up a poker game," suggested Mr. Talbot.

"You would suggest that, Benson," snapped his wife. "You know I perfectly loathe poker."

"I wouldn't mind learning how to play poker," said Marvel.

"I reckon we'd be glad to teach you," said Cory
Blaine with a wink at Talbot.

The buckboard that had brought Marvel had
also brought the mail, and after supper the news
of the day was the principal topic of conversation.

"Is there anything about the Gunderstrom
murder in your paper, Cory?" asked Dora Crowell, and then to Marvel, who was near her, "I
went to school with Mr. Gunderstrom's daughter
in Philadelphia."

"They haven't found that fellow Mason yet,"
said Blaine. "He's been missing for three weeks
— disappeared the day after the murder."

"You see," explained Dora to Marvel, "this
man Mason was a neighbor of Gunderstrom's,
and they'd been fighting over a piece of land for
nearly twenty years."

"And they think Mason killed him?" asked
Marvel.

"They know it," replied Dora. "A man called
up the sheriff's office on the telephone and told
them so."

"Mason was a deputy sheriff," explained Kay
White, "and he took advantage of his office to

pretend that he was looking for the murderer so that he could get away himself."

"Clever at that," commented Adams.

"A man who was well enough known to be a deputy sheriff ought not to be hard to find," commented Marvel.

"It says here in the paper," said Blaine, "that his horse showed up on the range a day or two ago; so that looks like he probably caught a train and beat it out of the country."

"He must be a terrible man," said Dora Crowell. "He shot poor Mr. Gunderstrom right through the heart as he lay asleep on his bed."

"Between the eyes," corrected Cory Blaine.

"It didn't say that in the paper," said Dora.

"Oh," said Blaine, "well, maybe it was in the heart."

Bruce Marvel rose. "What time are you starting in the morning?" he asked. "I think I'll be going to bed now."

"Breakfast at seven," said Blaine.

"Seven sharp," said Mr. Talbot.

"And we'll be leaving right after breakfast," said Blaine.

The entire party was assembled at the breakfast table when Bruce Marvel entered the dining room the following morning. Dora Crowell voiced an audible "My God" while Mrs. Talbot choked in an effort to control herself. Cory Blaine dissembled whatever surprise he felt, for it was his business not to notice the various eccentricities of dress evidenced by his guests, so long as they paid their bills.

"Good morning," said Marvel. "I'm sorry to be late, but I had trouble getting into my boots. My man usually helps me, you know."

No comment seemed to occur to anyone at the breakfast table; and so, amid silence, Marvel took his place between Kay White and Dora Crowell. He was arrayed in flagrantly new English riding boots, light tan English riding breeches, and a white polo shirt. But even more remarkable than his outfit was the fact that he did not seem to realize the incongruity of it. Apparently he was the only person at the breakfast table who was perfectly at ease.

If Cory Blaine realized the necessity of overlooking the foibles of his guests, his diplomacy was not always shared by the cowhands who herded the dudes on range; and when, shortly after breakfast, Bruce Marvel strode past the bunkhouse down toward the corrals he must need have been totally deaf to have missed all of the flippant remarks his sartorial effulgence precipitated.

The men were already leaving for the corrals to fetch up and saddle the horses, and Marvel soon had company.

"You aint aimin' to ride in them things, Mister, are you?" asked one of the men.

"That's what they were made for," replied Marvel.

"Them thar panties weren't never made to ride in. You can't tell me that," said a bow-legged puncher called Butts.

"You'll get 'em all dirty," opined another.

"And then what'll your mama say!" chimed in a third.

"They look funny to you, don't they?" asked Marvel good naturedly.

"They sure do, Mister," said Butts.

"That all depends upon who is doing the looking," said Marvel. "Did you ever look at yourself in a mirror?"

The other men laughed then at Butts' expense.

"What's wrong with me?" he demanded angrily.

"You're just funny looking," said Marvel with a laugh. "The only difference between us is that you don't know you're funny looking."

"It's a damn good thing for some of these dudes around here that they're guests," growled Butts.

"You needn't let that cramp your style any," said Marvel.

"Aw, cheese it," said one of the other men. "A guy's got a right to wear whatever he wants around here. It aint none of nobody's business."

"But there ought to be a law against them funny panties," vouchsafed another.

"You fellows talk too damn much," said a voice behind them. It was Cory Blaine, and he was scowling angrily. "Shake a leg now and get them horses caught up and saddled. We can't hang around here all day making funny cracks."

"Will you see that they get me a nice, gentle horse?" said Marvel.

"Sure, I'll fetch him up a nice, gentle one," said Butts. "There's old Crowhop, for instance."

"You ride Crowhop yourself," said Blaine. "Fetch up Baldy for Mr. Marvel. Baldy is all right," he said turning to his guest, "except that he always wants to take a few jumps the first thing in the morning. I'll top him for you myself, and after that he'll be as gentle as a kitten."

"Thanks," said Marvel. "I certainly shouldn't care to ride a bad horse."

"No, polo ponies don't buck, I guess," said Blaine.

iv

KAY WHITE

THE OTHER guests arrived at the corral by the time the horses were saddled, those who were going on the hunt being dressed, each according to his own ideas of what was either comfortable or proper. Bert Adams from Boston and Dora Crowell from Philadelphia might have crept out of the latest Western movie thriller. Mrs. Talbot, who also acted as unofficial chaperon, was resplendent in khaki knickers, white stockings, and high heeled laced shoes, with a silk shirtwaist, and coat to match her breeches, her only acknowledgment to the wild, wild west being a colored bandana tied about her neck and a Stetson hat, that was a size too small for her, perched on top of her bobbed locks. Benson Talbot was dressed for golf, while Kay White still clung to her overalls and workshirt, to which she had added a broad brimmed Stetson and a leather coat, for the chill of the Arizona night was still in the air.

As the cowhands led their horses out, Cory Blaine took Baldy from the corral and mounted him. The horse made a couple of jumps and then ran for a few hundred yards, after which he trotted docilely back to the corral.

Of course, every one had watched the topping of Baldy. Kay White was standing beside Marvel. "Isn't he a marvelous horseman," she said.

The man glanced quickly down at her. "Wonderful!" he said.

"He's perfectly safe now," said Blaine, reining in beside Marvel and dismounting.

"Thanks awfully," said Marvel. "But say, haven't you got an English saddle?"

Blaine looked at him with a pitying expression that he tried to conceal. "No, Mister," he said.

"I thought I'd ask," said Marvel. "You see I might not be able to ride in one of these cowboy saddles."

"Oh, you'll get used to it," said Kay. "I ride a flat saddle at home most of the time, but I found that if you can ride a flat saddle you can ride anything."

"I wish I had brought my own saddle," said Marvel.

"I'm glad he didn't," said Butts in a low tone to Dora Crowell. "He is sure funny enough now, and if he'd brung that I'd like as not have laughed myself to death."

"Perhaps he will be all right," said Dora, "when he becomes accustomed to our ways. He doesn't seem to be a half bad sort of a fellow."

"He's too fresh," said Butts.

Naturally all eyes were upon Marvel as he mounted Baldy. With few exceptions they were hoping that the horse would pitch a little, but he did not. Marvel mounted a little awkwardly, caught his knee on the cantle of the saddle and then sat on it, afterward slipping down into the seat. He also appeared to have trouble in finding his right hand stirrup.

"Good bye, Kay, and be careful of snakes," called Miss Pruell to her niece, as the party moved away, "and please be sure that she has enough covers at night, Mrs. Talbot."

"Good bye, Aunt Abbie," called the girl. "I wish you were coming with us."

"Heaven forbid!" exclaimed Miss Pruell. "It is quite bad enough here, without riding horseback all day in search of further discomfort."

"Your aunt has a lot of sense," said Marvel; "a lot more than we have."

"You don't expect to have a good time then?" she asked.

"I wouldn't say that exactly," he said, his eyes upon her fresh, young beauty, "but at that nobody with good sense would choose to sleep on the ground if he could sleep in a bed."

"Oh, you'll like it after you get used to it," she told him.

"Perhaps," was his only comment.

Presently Blaine broke into a trot; and as the others took up the gait, Marvel forged a little ahead of Kay White and she noted, to her dismay, that he rode awkwardly; in fact, his form seemed almost an exact replica of that adopted by Birdie Talbot, who rode just ahead of him. It seemed a pity, she thought; he was so nice looking. His smooth, sunburned face and clear eyes suggested a life spent much out of doors; and when she had seen him in his riding clothes she had been quite certain that he would prove himself a good horseman, in spite of the incongruity of his apparel.

"How am I doing?" he asked, as she moved up to his side.

"Will you mind if I tell you?" she asked.

"Certainly not. I'd like to have you."

"Then, hold your reins in your left hand," she said, "and don't lean forward so much."

"That is the new army seat," he explained.

"I can't help what it is. I don't like it," she said. "Let your feet hang naturally. Don't carry them back, and whatever you do don't try to post in a stock saddle. Your stirrups are much too long for that, and besides they are not far enough forward."

"I'm riding just like Mrs. Talbot," he said.

"Well for heaven's sake, don't copy her. She

was never on a horse before in her life until she came here two weeks ago."

"Is this better?"

"Keep your seat.   Don't bounce so."

"I'm trying not to," he said.

"Look at that damn dude," said Butts to one of the other cowhands, who was riding with him in rear of the party.   "Polo, my foot!   I don't believe that guy ever seen a horse before."

"Him and Birdie must have takin' riding lessons from the same correspondence school," said his companion.

"Well, Birdie is a woman; and you can't expect nuthin' from them," said Butts, "but it sure gives me a pain to see anything that calls itself a man ride like that."

"They is all a bunch of freaks," said the other. "I'd sure hate to have my poor old paw see me with this outfit."

"Look at Bert ride.   I'll bet he's got corns now."

"When he gets back to Boston he'll have to eat off the mantlepiece."

"Well, I don't mind the others so much," said Butts.   "I got kinda used to 'em; but that dude that blew in last night, him and me aint goin' to be no pals. Every time I look at his panties I want to hit him."

"Why don't you then? He invited you to."

"I can't on Cory's account. We got to treat a payin' customer decent whether we like him or not. But I'm goin' to get that guy just the same, only he won't know who done it."

"I never took no college degree," replied his companion, "but if I know anything, I know enough not to monkey with a guy with eyes like that dude."

"Looks don't mean nuthin' with them Eastern dudes," said Butts; "that's all they got."

For three days the party rode deeper into a wilderness of mountains and meadows until they reached their destination, a tiny shack beside a leaping trout stream in a valley hemmed by lofty mountains, where lived Hi Bryam, the owner of four good lion dogs that the party was to use in the forthcoming hunt. The chuck wagon had met them at Mill Creek and had been able to accompany them as far as Bryam's.

Beyond this point there was no wagon road; but lion were known to be plentiful in the mountains all about them, and Blaine had planned that they were to arrange their hunts from this camp so that they could return at night.

Before they had reached Bryam's, Bruce Marvel was well acquainted with his companions; and had found them a democratic and likeable lot, who had cast aside all formalities, including titles and surnames.

An instinctive diffidence had made it difficult for him to call the women by their first names; but he had finally been badgered into it, though it still required a distinct moral effort to call the fat Mrs. Talbot Birdie. Kay and Dora came much more easily to his lips — especially Kay. The girl from Philadelphia seemed rather mannish to him; but Kay White, in spite of her overalls and self reliance, was essentially feminine. During the long rides and the evenings in camp he had learned much concerning her and the other members of the party. He had learned, for instance, though not from Kay, that her father was a wealthy California banker; that her mother was dead and that shortly after the lion hunt, she expected her father to join her at the home ranch.

He had also surmised from what he had seen

that Cory Blaine was much interested in Kay White; and that troubled him, for he did not like Blaine. There was something about the man that made Marvel think he was playing a part and that he was not at all at heart what he appeared to be. Butts, who seemed to be Blaine's right hand man, remained tacitly antagonistic to Marvel; but Bud, the other cowhand who accompanied the party, was inclined to be friendly.

Toward Hi Bryam he conceived an immediate and instinctive dislike. The fellow was tall and lanky, with a peculiarly repellent face and a surly manner that invited no familiarities.

Three days of hunting brought no success; and on the fourth day Marvel found himself paired off with Dora Crowell, while Blaine and Kay White followed him. Hi Bryam, with the other two dogs, led Dora and Bruce along the opposite ridge, the parties joining where the two ridges met some ten miles above camp. Bert Adams, sore and lame, remained in camp with the Talbots.

Cory Blaine was unusually silent as he led the way up the steep and rocky trail toward the summit of the ridge, and even when they stopped occasionally on some leveler and more favorable spot to blow their horses he seemed strangely pre-occupied.

"You seem worried this morning, Cory," observed the girl, as they halted again, this time near the summit of the ridge.

"I reckon I am," said the man.

"What's the matter?"

"I'm worried because I'm such an ignorant cuss," said Blaine.

The girl laughed lightly. "What makes you think you're ignorant?" she demanded.

"You know I am," he said. "I aint got no book learning."

"You are far from ignorant," she told him. "There is a lot of knowledge in the world that is not in any book. Some of the most ignorant people in the world are scholars."

"That seems funny," he said. "But maybe ignorant aint the word I mean. What I mean is that I don't know how to do and say things the way, well, Bert Adams does, for instance. He's what they call a gentleman, and I'm not. I got sense enough to see that."

"It takes something more than a knowledge of

English to constitute a gentleman, Cory," she told him.

"Yes, I suppose so," he agreed; "but there is a difference that I can't explain. I know it's there, and you know it's there. I'm not the same as you and Dora Crowell and Bert Adams. I'm not the kind that you people would associate with."

"Why how could you say that, Cory Blaine?" she exclaimed. "Has any one of us said or done anything to make you think that he thought he was better than you?"

"Of course not; but nevertheless you know it, and I know it."

"Nonsense."

"There aint no nonsense about it, Kay;" insisted the man, "and I could prove it."

"How?"

"By asking you one question."

"What is it?" Instantly the words were spoken she regretted them, but it was too late.

"Would you marry a feller like me?"

"Don't be foolish," she said. "How in the world does a girl know whom she will marry?"

"But you wouldn't marry any ignorant cow puncher?" he insisted.

"I don't know," she said. "I suppose that I am no different from any other woman. If I loved a man, I would not care what he was — I mean that I would marry him no matter what he was."

"But you would rather that he wouldn't be an ignorant cow puncher?" he insisted.

"I don't see why you keep harping on that," she said. "It isn't fair, Cory."

"Well," he said, "I've got my answer."

"What do you mean by that?"

"I mean that you've told me that you'd never marry an ignorant cow puncher."

"I've told you nothing of the kind. I'd marry Hi Bryam if I loved him."

The man relapsed into silence as they started again along the trail. The girl was troubled. She was sorry that he had spoken, for she knew now what was in his heart; but she did not know her own.

Kay White was a normal young woman. She had been attracted by other men in the past, but her compulsion at such times had never been of such a nature as to convince her that she had been in love. She conceived of love as a devastating passion, compelling and unreasoning; and certainly no man had ever aroused such an emotion in her breast; but she realized that perhaps she might be mistaken, and she also realized that she had been undeniably attracted toward Cory Blaine. That love might start this way she had little doubt, but inwardly she shrank from the thought that she might love Blaine.

As she recalled their recent conversation she realized that she was now not at all sure that she had actually meant what she said. The statement that she would marry Hi Bryam if she loved him had been an emotional nonsensicality, and this admission raised the question as to whether she would marry Cory Blaine if she loved him.

She was not a snob, but she was endowed with more than an average amount of good sense. She had known some and heard of many girls who trod the same walk of life as she who had married stable managers or chauffeurs; and very few of these matches had turned out happily, not because of the positions that the men held, but because everything in their training and environment and in the training and environment of their friends had been so different from that to which the girls had been accustomed that neither could find comfort nor happiness in the social sphere of the other.

The result of this thoughtful deliberation was to arouse regret for the statements that she had made; for she saw that they might, in a way, be construed as encouraging a hope within his breast; and that he might harbor such a hope seemed evident not only by his words but by the many attentions he had shown her since she had come to the TF Ranch.

But had he not also been attentive to Dora Crowell? Perhaps it was Dora he wanted, and perhaps he had only been sounding her to ascertain the attitude of a girl in a social sphere similar to that to which Dora belonged. Kay wondered, and as she considered the matter she also wondered if she would be pleased or disappointed should this prove to be a correct interpretation of his motives.

Where the trail widened again Blaine drew rein. "We'll rest here a minute," he said, and as she stopped her horse beside him he reached out and seized her hand. "I love you, Kay," he said. "Don't you think you could learn to love me?"

"I have been thinking about that for the last few minutes, Cory," she replied, "and I shall be perfectly honest with you. I do not want to love you. Please do not say anything more about it."

"I am going to make you love me," he said.

V

THE LION HUNT

AS THEIR ponies climbed up the steep acclivity toward the summit of the hogback along which Bryam and his hounds had preceded them, Dora Crowell and Bruce Marvel paused occasionally to rest their mounts and to pursue one of those disjointed conversations that are peculiar to mountain trails.

"I think you're riding better every day, Bruce," said the girl. "If you stay here long enough you ought to make a horseman."

The man smiled. "Perhaps I'd do better if I had my own saddle," he said.

"Now don't be silly, Bruce. A flat saddle is all right in the park, but it would look perfectly ridiculous here."

"Can you rope?" he asked.

"Of course not. Why?" she demanded.

"Then what good is that heavy frame and the big horn on your saddle to you?" he asked.

"Don't be disagreeable," she said.

"I'm not trying to be disagreeable," he told her. "I'm just trying to find out."

"Find out what?"

"Why it would be silly to put a light saddle on your horse and not make him carry twenty-five or thirty pounds extra all day over rough, steep trails."

"What do they have these saddles for then?" she demanded.

"They have them for cowmen to use in their business. They have to be strong enough to hold a wild bull, and nobody needs one unless he can rope and hold a wild creature and expects to have to do it. I'll tell you, Dora, there are a lot of fellows wearing chaps and ten gallon hats who have no business weighting their horses down with a stock saddle and a rope that they wouldn't know how to use if they had to."

"There are a lot of false alarms in the world," she admitted. "I am one myself with all this cowboy scenery; but everyone knows it, including myself; so I am not deceiving anyone, but if I am a false alarm I am not the only one."

"No?"

"No. There is at least one other. He may fool the rest of them, but he doesn't fool me."

"The world is full of false alarms," he said.

"But if people are going to try that they should know every little detail well enough to get away with it."

"Like you posing as a cowgirl," he grinned.

"Or you posing as an Eastern polo player," she retorted.

"Why?" he asked innocently. "What makes you think that of me?"

"There are several things, but one is enough. You have your boot garters on backward."

"I always was careless," he said.

"That's not carelessness, Bruce. That's ignorance, and you know it."

"You couldn't expect me to come out here on a cattle ranch and admit that I'd never seen a horse before, could you?" he demanded.

"You've seen plenty of horses before," she told him. "You may be a good actor, but you're not quite good enough for me. I might not have guessed it, except for the boot garters, before to-day; but after riding up this mountain behind you where I could watch every move you made, I know."

"What did you expect me to do, fall off?" he asked.

"It's none of my business, Bruce; and I won't say anything more about it. I'm just one of those persons who hate to have anyone think that he is putting anything over on her."

"This isn't hunting mountain lion," he said, and they rode on.

When, at last, they reached the trail that ran along the summit of the hogback, he drew rein again; and as the girl rode up, he pointed across the canyon to the summit of the opposite ridge. "There's Kay and Blaine," he said. "Which one of them is a false alarm? It's not her, I'm sure of that."

"These Western clothes are nothing new to her," said Dora. "Her father owns ranches in California; and she has ridden all her life, Western and English both. It's funny," she added, "how so many of us want to be something else beside what we really are, and after all Kay is no better than the rest of us."

"How's that?" he asked.

"You don't think that she wears overalls and blue work shirts at home, do you?" she demanded.

"Well, now, really, I hadn't thought about it;" he replied, "but she certainly looks mighty cute in them."

"If she had to wear overalls at home she'd be crazy to go somewhere where she could wear fine clothes. There's a little false alarm in all of us. I remember a girl at school like that. Do you recall the night you came to the ranch? We were talking about the murder of a man by the name of Gunderstrom in New Mexico?"

"Yes," he said.

"Well, this girl I'm speaking of was Gunderstrom's daughter. She was about the sweetest and most natural girl I had ever met when she

came to the school that I was attending just outside of Philadelphia.   She was typically Western; but after awhile she seemed to get ashamed
of that and became a regular false alarm, not only
in her clothes, but in her manners and her speech.
Then last year we roomed together; and I grew
very fond of her, though I am afraid she is still a
false alarm in some respects and always will be."

"Just what do you mean?" he asked.

"I mean that she is trying to pretend to be
something that she was not born to be."

"I see," he said.

"Perhaps it was her father's fault.   She told
me that he would not let her come West after he
sent her back East to school.   He wanted her to
be a fine lady and to forget everything connected
with her childhood.   I know, though, that at
many times she was homesick for the West; and
when I heard of her father's death and telegraphed my condolences, I suggested that she
come out here to the TF Ranch and spend the
rest of the summer with me."

"Is she coming?" asked Marvel, his casual
tone masking his eagerness.

"She wired that she was going home first and

that if she found that she could get away, she would come."

Their conversation was interrupted by the baying of the hounds far ahead. "They've raised a lion," he said. "We'd better be moving."

The girl, thrilled and excited by the prospect of being in at a kill, spurred her horse into a gallop and brushed past him on the trail. "Careful, Dora," he called after her. "This is no place to run a horse unless you have to."

"Come on," she called back, "I don't want to miss anything." But evidently he did not share her excitement for he moved on slowly at a walk.

His head was bowed in thought, which, however, had nothing to do with lions. Presently he glanced down at his legs, first at one, then at the other; and then presently he reached down and unbuckled one of his boot garters, removed it, held it up and looked at it. After a moment of silent scrutiny, he held it down against his leg, turning it first one way and then another. Then he shook his head sadly and threw it off into the brush, after which he removed the other and threw that away also.

When he finally came up with the rest of the

party they were all gathered around a tree in which a mountain lion had come to bay. Kay and Cory were there with Bryam and Butts and the four hounds. They were trying to decide who should have the honor of shooting the quarry.

"Let both girls shoot at him at the same time," said Blaine, "and Hi can be ready to plug him if they miss."

"I don't care anything about shooting him," said Kay White. "I'd much rather see him alive. Doesn't he look free and wild and splendid?"

"He just looks like a deer killer to me," said Hi Bryam. "If it warn't for them sons-o'-guns, we'd have plenty of deer in these hills."

"Like they have in the Kaibab forest," said Kay, "since they killed off all the lions — so many deer that there isn't food enough for them and they're starving to death."

"Well if Kay doesn't want to shoot him, I do," said Dora.

She had already dismounted and stood ready with her rifle. Bryam was pointing out the best location for the shot and just where to stand to get the aim she wanted.

The others lolled in their saddles as Dora raised her rifle to her shoulder and took careful aim. At the sharp report of the weapon the horses all started nervously. Kay's mount wheeled and jumped away; and as she sought to control him, one of her reins parted; and the frightened animal broke into a run down the rough summit of the ridge.

The horror of the situation must have been instantly apparent to every member of the party; for the narrow trail, rocky in places, winding among the scant, low brush, offered precarious footing to a walking horse carefully picking his way along, while further down it dropped steeply and eventually pitched into the canyon at so steep an angle that even a walking horse, going most carefully, might be lost if he stumbled.

All of these thoughts flashed through the minds of the men and the girl, who, apparently, were utterly helpless to avert the inevitable disaster toward which Kay's horse was carrying her; yet almost at the instant that her horse bolted, Marvel put spurs to his own mount and, shaking the reins loose, gave him his head in pursuit.

"The damn fool!" exclaimed Cory Blaine.

"He'll kill her and himself, too. Chasing him will only make that fool pony run faster. God, why did I bring that damn dude along?"

Whatever the outcome, nothing that they might do now could save them; so the entire party followed, forgetful of the dead lion and the worrying hounds.

Baldy was swift, and for that Marvel offered up a silent prayer of thanks. The man paid no attention to the trail, holding his horse straight after the flying pony, Baldy taking the low bushes in his strides, his iron shoes striking fire from the dangerous rocks.

He was gaining; and then he stumbled and nearly fell, but recovered himself and was away again.

"Stay with him, Kay," shouted the man. "I'm coming."

She recognized his voice; and her heart sank, for she had no confidence in his horsemanship nor in his ability in a crisis such as this. She wondered where Cory was, for she knew that Cory could have saved her.

Baldy was closing the distance between them. Now his nose was at the rump of the runaway.

Marvel held him to a parallel course that he might come up on the near side of Kay's mount. A higher bush intervened, around which the trail swerved, but Marvel held his horse straight for the obstacle. A low word of encouragement, a light touch of the spur and Baldy cleared the bush; nor did he lose his stride, and now his nose was at Kay's knees.

"Get ready!" said the man to the girl, and again his spurs touched Baldy's side and he spoke in his flattened ears.

Great with courage is the heart of a good horse, and few there are that will fail a man in a crisis; nor did Baldy fail, and his next jump took him abreast of the runaway.

Marvel encircled Kay's waist. "Put your arms around my neck," he said, "and kick your feet free of the stirrups." Then he straightened up and lifted her out of the saddle and spoke quietly to Baldy as he reined him in, while the runaway, in his next jump, stumbled and fell, rolling over and over before he came to rest, stunned and prostrate.

Baldy, thoroughly excited by the race, seemed little inclined to stop; and for a while it looked to those behind and to the girl clinging to the man's neck that, handicapped as he was, he would be unable to control him; but at last the great bit and the strength of the rider prevailed, and Baldy came to a stop, trembling and blowing.

Gently Marvel lowered the girl to the ground. Then he dismounted and walked around his horse to her side. She was trembling; and there were tears in her eyes; and he put his arm about her again to support her, for she seemed to be about to fall.

"All in?" he asked.

"Pretty much," she replied.

"I'll look after your horse myself after this," he said. "This would never have happened if any one had been watching him."

"I don't know what to say to you," she said. "It seems so silly to try to thank anyone for such a thing."

"If you want to thank anyone," he said, "thank Baldy. That is sure some pony. I knew he was fast. I could tell that after I saw him run every morning when they topped him for me; and I guessed that he had the heart, too. These horses that like to play usually have plenty of heart."

"I think you were the one that had the heart," she said; "for you knew that at any minute you might be killed, but Baldy didn't know that."

"Those things sure happen fast," he said. "A man doesn't have any time to think. Hold Baldy a second while I go over and have a look at that horse of yours."

She took the reins; and as he walked back toward the animal that was still lying where he had fallen she followed behind him.

The other members of the party were riding up, and they all met close to Kay's pony.

The animal lay on its side, breathing heavily, its legs outstretched. Marvel's first glance at it convinced him that none of its legs was broken. Blood was running from a small cut in the top of the animal's head; but he did not appear to be badly injured in any way, only too stunned, or perhaps too frightened to try to arise.

Marvel seized the broken bridle reins and urged the horse to get up; and as he scrambled to his feet, it was apparent that he was far from being crippled.

"Why he's not hurt much at all, is he?" exclaimed Kay.

"These cow ponies are pretty tough babies," said Marvel. "You'd have to hit this fellow with an axe to knock him out, and you'd be lucky if you didn't break the axe."

Dora and Cory had dismounted and walked over to Kay. Dora threw her arms about the girl and kissed her. "Lord! Kay," she exclaimed, "I guess I was worse scared than you;" then she sat down in the dirt and commenced to cry.

The men had gathered around Kay's pony, which seemed to offer some relief from their embarrassed silence. Blaine did not look at Marvel; for he was recalling his disparaging prophecy of a few moments before, while Butts was trying to convince himself that the dude's success had been only a matter of accident. Hi Bryam took a fresh chew and remounted his horse.

"I reckon I'll ride back after the dogs," he said. "Butts can come along and give me a lift with the lion, if it's still there. I seen it fall all right, but by golly I don't know whether it was killed or not."

As Butts mounted and followed Bryam, Marvel led Kay's pony down the trail a few yards and then back again.

"He's all right," he said. Then he fastened the broken end of the bridle rein to the bit with a peculiar knot that went unnoticed by all but Cory Blaine. He looked to the stirrups and the cinches next, loosening the latter and settling the saddle into its proper place with a shake. "Good as new," he said, as he tightened the cinches again.

"You are not going to ride him again, Kay, are you?" asked Dora.

Marvel was untying the coiled neck rope from the pommel of Kay's saddle. "You can ride him," he said, "but I'm going to lead him."

"That's a rather humiliating way to ride into camp," said Kay.

"But safe," said Marvel. "He's still scared." And so they returned to camp with few breaks in the silence that the exigencies of the trail and their moods induced.

Cory Blaine had ridden in moody silence. He had scarcely spoken a word since the accident. He was helping Bud with the horses now; and as he swung the saddles across the pole of the chuck wagon and turned the horses loose to graze, he seemed buried in a brown study. When the last horse had trotted away, he took the broken bridle from the horn of Kay's saddle and examined it closely. "Look at this, Bud," he said presently. "Did you ever see a paper collared, cracker fed dude that could tie a knot like that?"

"No," said Bud, after examining Marvel's handiwork.

"Neither did I," said Blaine; "and you should see the son-of-a-gun ride," he spat with disgust; "and I've been topping his horse for him every morning."

"What's his game?"

"I wish I knew," said Cory Blaine.

vi

HI BRYAM

THE TWO girls had gone to their tent and thrown themselves upon their blankets to rest, exhausted as much perhaps by the excitement through which they had passed as by the fatigue of the long ride. For a long time they lay there in silence, thinking. Kay was trying to piece together the jumbled impressions of those few harrowing minutes during which she had felt death spurring swiftly at her elbow. She recalled her disappointment when she had realized that it was

Bruce Marvel and not Cory Blaine who was riding to her rescue, and she lived again the instant when a strong arm had gone about her body and quiet words of instruction had been spoken in her ear. In that instant she had known that she was safe; and as she had clung to him, her arms about his neck, she had sensed the strength of the man and his ability to protect her. What he had done he had done so quietly and coolly that it was difficult to believe that this was the same man who had been the object of the good-natured pity of them all.

"You've heard of people losing ten years growth in a second, haven't you?" said Dora out of the silence. "Well, I lost twenty when I saw your horse bolt and realized that he was uncontrollable. Were you terribly frightened?"

"Yes, I was," replied Kay frankly. "I didn't lose my head; and I recall now that I figured out in the first few seconds what my chances were, and they didn't seem very good. I know I made up my mind that before I'd let him carry me over the edge into the ravine, I would jump; but I hoped that he might stop, for I knew that I should be hurt terribly if I jumped. I was most afraid of his falling; that trail is terribly rough."

"I don't see how Bruce's horse ever kept his feet," said Dora. "He wasn't following any trail. Bruce just rode straight, jumping everything."

"He is wonderful," said Kay simply, "and this morning we were kidding him because he let Cory top Baldy for him. I don't understand him."

"You'd understand him a whole lot less if you had been riding behind him instead of in front of him," said Dora.

"Why?" asked Kay.

"He rode as though he was a part of Baldy. I've been around horsemen all my life, and I guess you have, too, Kay; and we both know that there is something in the way a man sits his saddle that proclaims him either a horseman or a dub at first glance."

"But I have seen him ride for the last several days," said Kay, "and he certainly hasn't impressed me as being anything but an amateur. You know that some times, under the stress of an emergency, a person can do things that he could not do otherwise."

"Slush!" exclaimed Dora. "I watched him

riding while we were alone this morning; and I guess he must have forgotten himself for the time being, and I saw then that he could ride. And when he rode after you, Kay — why, my dear, it was magnificent. And not only the way he sat his horse, but the way he controlled him."

"He is terribly strong, too," said Kay reminiscently. "He lifted me out of the saddle as though I didn't weigh anything."

"Do you know," said Dora, "that there is something peculiar about him? I don't believe that he is what he claims to be at all."

"What does he claim to be?" asked Kay. "I've never heard him talk about himself."

"Well, that's right, too. He hasn't exactly claimed to be anything; but his clothes and his reference to polo and yachting and literature do, in a way, constitute a sort of indirect claim to a certain position in life; but every once in awhile he slips, usually in his English; or again by the use of a colloquialism that is not of the East, where he certainly has tried to give us the impression he is from."

"Well, what do you suppose his purpose is?"

"I think he is a joker," replied Dora. "He is

having a fine time all by himself making monkeys of us."

"Oh, girls," interrupted Birdie Talbot, bursting into their tent. "Here comes Butts and Mr. Bryam with Dora's lion."

For the next few minutes the lion held the center of the stage. It was propped up and photographed with Dora standing beside it with her rifle. It was stretched out and measured, and then it was photographed again while Dora stood with one foot upon it.

"You made a bully shot," said Cory Blaine.

"Right through the heart," said Butts.

"Could you kill a lion with a revolver, Blaine?" asked Bruce Marvel.

"Sure, if you could hit him," replied Cory.

"I guess it would take a pretty good revolver shot to hit him in the heart," said Marvel, "but I suppose you're a pretty good shot."

"Nothing extra," said Blaine modestly.

"I'd like to try my hand with one of those some time," said Marvel. "Do you mind if I took a couple of shots with yours? I could put a tin can up over there against that tree."

"Hop to it if you want to," said Blaine. He

took his gun from its holster and handed it to Marvel. "Be careful," he said, "that you don't shoot yourself."

Marvel took the weapon gingerly, walked over past the chuck wagon, where his bedroll lay and laid the weapon on top of the roll. Then he found an empty can which he placed at the foot of the tree, about twenty yards distant.

"Two bits says you can't hit it in five shots," said Butts.

"I'll take that," said Bruce. "I certainly ought to hit it once in five times."

As he picked the weapon up from his bedroll, it went off prematurely. "Gosh," he said, "I only touched the trigger."

"I told you to be careful," snapped Cory. "You're lucky you didn't shoot your foot off."

"I shot a hole in my bed," said Bruce. "I'll pay you for the damage to the blanket though, Blaine, when we get back to the ranch."

"Be careful how you handle it now and don't aim it this way," cautioned Cory.

"There's five shots left," said Butts. "See if you can hit the can once."

The rest of the party had moved forward

now, and all were watching interestedly. Birdie Talbot offered to bet a dollar on Bruce's marksmanship.

"Want to bet, Cory?" she asked.

Blaine was watching Marvel through narrowed lids. "No," he said. Perhaps he was recalling the man's unexpectedly developed horsemanship.

"I'll take a dollar's worth," said her husband.

"That's right," said Dora. "Keep it in the family."

Marvel took careful aim and fired.

"Miss number one," gloated Butts.

"He is not familiar with that gun," said Kay.

"Nor no other," said Butts.

Marvel shot again four times, scoring four clean misses.

"He didn't even hit the tree," chortled Butts, happily.

"I wasn't shooting at the tree," said Marvel. "I was shooting at the can. Here's your two bits, Butts." Then he handed the weapon back to Blaine. "I guess it must take a lot of practice," he said.

"Well," said Birdie Talbot, disgustedly, "I

don't see how anybody could miss that can five times in succession."

"I didn't either," said Marvel.

"Come on, Birdie, pay up," said her husband, "and don't be a poor loser."

"Try and collect," said Mrs. Talbot.

"That's what you get for betting with your wife," laughed Dora Crowell.

Talbot laughed. "I win anyway," he said, "for if anyone else had taken her up, I would have had to pay."

Marvel had unrolled his blankets and was looking at them ruefully. "Why here is the bullet," he exclaimed. "It didn't go all the way through. I'll have to keep it as a reminder of my marksmanship;" and he slipped it into his pocket.

After supper that night, Marvel strolled over to Bryam's camp, where the hunter was sitting upon his doorstep, puffing on his pipe. Bryam had shown no desire to associate with the members of the hunting party; nor was there anything about his manner to invite friendly advances, but Marvel seemed unabashed by the surly expression upon the man's face.

"Good evening," he said.

Bryam grunted.

"It must get lonesome up here alone," observed Marvel.

"Must it?"

"What do you do to pass away the time?" persisted the younger man.

"It takes about all of my time minding my own business," growled Bryam.

Apparently unaffected by these rebuffs, Marvel seated himself upon the doorstep at the hunter's side. In the silence that followed Bryam puffed intermittently at his pipe, while Marvel bent his eyes upon the ground in thought.

Hi Bryam, he concluded, was a peculiar man, certainly hard to get acquainted with; and he saw that he was peculiar physically, too, as he noted the size of the man's boots. Surreptitiously he placed his own beside one of them. There was fully an inch and a half difference between them in length.

"Many lion up here?" asked Marvel presently.

"Not as many as there was this morning," said Bryam.

There followed a considerable silence. "It

must be quiet up here nights," suggested Marvel.

"It is when there aint some damn fool shooting off his face," replied the hunter.

Again there was a long silence. "You got a nice cabin," said Marvel.

"Have I?"

Marvel rose. "You mind if I look in it?" he said. "I'd like to see the inside of a hunter's cabin."

Bryam rose and stood in the doorway. "There aint nuthin' in here to interest you," he said. "You better run along to bed now."

"Well, may be you're right," said Marvel. "Good night, and thank you for the pleasant evening."

Bryam made no reply, and Marvel walked back to the campfire where the other members of the party were gathered. "We were just wondering where you were," said Birdie Talbot.

"Thought you'd wandered off and lost yourself," said Butts.

"No, I was just calling on Mr. Bryam," said Marvel.

"I hope you enjoyed your visit," said Blaine.

"Very much indeed," replied Marvel.

"Bryam must have changed then," said Butts. "He wouldn't aim to entertain no tenderfoot if he knew it. He aint got much use for 'em."

"He didn't know it," said Marvel. He moved off toward his blankets. "Good night, folks," he said. "I'm going to turn in."

"I just naturally don't like that fellow," said Butts, when Marvel was out of earshot.

"Then keep it to yourself," snapped Blaine, rising. "I think you'd all better turn in if we want to get an early start in the morning."

When the others had retired to their tents and blankets, Blaine and Butts made their way to Bryam's cabin, the interior of which was faintly lighted by a single oil lamp standing upon a rough table where Bryam was playing solitaire with a deck of greasy cards.

As the two men entered the shack, a shadow seemed to move among the denser shadows of the pine trees, to come to rest opposite an open window.

"I won't get another chance to talk with you before we leave in the morning, Hi," said Blaine; "and I want to be sure there aint goin' to be no misunderstanding. Mart and Eddie know just what to do. When they get here, keep 'em one night; and let 'em rest. Get an early start the next morning. Take the south trail to the summit, and then follow the One Mile Creek trail around into Sonora. Eddie and Mart know the trail to Kelly's place from there on. They just been down there and got it fixed up with the old man; and remember this, Hi, no funny business and no rough stuff. If you pull anything raw, I'll croak you sure; and that goes for Mart and Eddie and Kelly; and they know it, too."

Bryam grunted. "I aint crazy yet," he said.

vii

The Bur

It was a cold morning that broke fair and beautiful as the hunters struck their camp. The horses felt the cinches with humped backs. Baldy was even more convex than usual.

"Aren't you going to top him for me this morning, Blaine?" asked Marvel, as Cory started to mount his own horse.

"I guess you don't need nobody to top your horses for you," said Blaine shortly.

"He looks like he was going to buck for sure this morning," said Marvel.

"I'll top him for you, Mister," said Butts.

"Thanks," said Marvel. "I certainly don't want to get an arm or leg broken way up here in the mountains."

"Here, hold my horse," said Butts.

He swung gently into Marvel's saddle; and, true to form, Baldy took two or three jumps and bolted for a few hundred yards. Butts rode him on a little farther, and those at the camp saw him dismount and pick something up from the ground. Then he remounted and returned to camp at a lope.

"What did you find?" asked Marvel.

"Oh, I thought I seen something," said Butts, "but I didn't." He dismounted and looked to Baldy's cinches, readjusting the saddle and straightening out the blanket back of the cantle, raising the skirt of the saddle to do so; then he turned the horse over to Marvel, but it was noticeable to all that Baldy had more of a hump now than before. In fact, he was moving about nervously, and seemed to be of a mind to start bucking before he was mounted.

As Butts threw his leg over his own horse, he winked at Bud. "It ought to be a large mornin'," he said.

Marvel raised the skirt of his saddle and reached under the blanket. When he withdrew his hand he held it out to Butts. "This yours?" he asked, and opening his hand he revealed a bur.

Butts tried to look innocent. "What do you mean?" he asked.

"Oh, nothing," said Marvel, dropping the bur to the ground and mounting Baldy, from whose back the hump had immediately disappeared with the removal of the bur.

The day's ride was to include an excursion to a point of scenic interest that would profitably occupy the time of the mounted members of the party while the chuck wagon was moving by a more direct route to the next camp.

As they started out, Cory Blaine succeeded in pairing himself off with Kay White. The Talbots rode together, as did Bud and Butts, leaving Dora and Bruce as companions of the trail. Bert Adams rode ignominiously in the chuck wagon.

"Well, how is the mysterious Mr. Marvel this morning?" asked the girl.

"Just as mysterious as an old shoe," he replied.

"Or a ladder," she suggested.

"I think you must be one of those writer folks," he said.

"What makes you think that?"

"You're just hell bent on making a story out of nothing."

"Now don't disappoint me," she said. "I am thrilled to death with mysteries in real life."

"Well, you just go on thrilling while you can, Dora," he said with a laugh; "for you're going to find that a tired business man, off on his vacation, aint much of a range to hunt thrills on."

"Meaning Benson Talbot?" she asked.

"There's not a thrill in him," said Dora; "but he's the only business man in the outfit."

"How do you reckon I live, then?" he asked.

"I don't know," she said, "but if you're a business man, I'm a cowgirl."

"I don't wonder you're suspicious," he said.

"Why?" she demanded.

"I've been reading a lot about politics in Pennsylvania, and I shouldn't blame you if you didn't trust nobody."

"There you go again," she said.

"Go again?   What do you mean?"

"When you are off your guard your English slips."

He flushed slightly.   "Maybe that comes from associating with cowgirls and other illiterate people," he said.

"And maybe that also accounts for the fact that although you are supposed to be a tender-foot, you knew immediately this morning that Butts had put a bur under Baldy's saddle."

"Oh, pshaw," he said, "anybody could see that."

"I didn't," she said, "and I was just as near to him as you."

"Maybe I am more observing," he suggested.

"Oh, not so very," she told him, "or you wouldn't have put your boot garters on back-wards.   By the way, where are they?"

"I reckon they fell off yesterday when I was chasing Kay's pony."

"Why don't you tell the truth?" she demanded. "You couldn't figure them out, and so you threw them away."

"I always did think they were silly things," he said.   "I never wear them at home."

"I'll bet you never did. Come on, Bruce, 'fess up. You're not what you pretend to be, are you?"

"I don't know what you think I am," he said; "but perhaps it's a good thing that I am not whatever it is, for I have heard tell that in this part of the country curiosity was sometimes a very fatal disease."

He smiled as he spoke, but the girl caught an undertone of seriousness that sobered her. "Forgive me," she said. "I have been impossible, but really I meant nothing by it. I didn't wish to pry into your private affairs."

"That's all right, Dora," he said with a laugh, "and you needn't be afraid. I'm not going to knife you in the back."

"No," she said, "I know you wouldn't; but I should hate to get too curious about Butts, or even Cory Blaine."

"Why?" he asked.

"I don't know," she replied. "Perhaps it is just a woman's intuition."

"Well, you must have seen a lot of them," he said. "You've been here some time, haven't you?"

"Yes," she answered, "I have; but they have not always been here all the time. They go away occasionally, some times for a week or ten days, Cory's looking after cattle interests."

"He has cattle interests?" asked Marvel.

"And a mine, too, he says," replied Dora.

"Well, he hasn't been looking after them much lately," said Marvel.

"They got back from a trip about three weeks before you came to the ranch," she said; "and it must have been a hard one, too, for they were all in for a couple of days afterward. I guess Cory's a pretty hard rider, too. His horse dropped dead in the corral the morning they got in from that last trip. Bud told me about it."

"Wasn't Bud with them?" asked Marvel.

"No, he stays here and sort of looks after the dude ranch for Cory while he is away."

"Bud seems to be a pretty nice fellow."

"Yes, he is a nice boy," said the girl. "Everybody likes Bud."

They rode on for a while in silence that was finally broken by the girl. "I can't understand why it is," she said, "that I have that peculiar feeling about Cory Blaine. He has always been

pleasant and accommodating, but away down inside somewhere I don't seem to be able to trust
him. What do you think of him, Bruce?"

"Oh, I have no reason to have anything against
him," replied the man. "He's always been decent
enough to me, though it has probably been hard
work for him to be decent to a tenderfoot."

"You can't have much use for Butts though; he
has certainly been nasty enough to you."

"Butts is like having fleas," he replied. "They
may annoy you, but you can't really hate them.
A thing's got to have brains before a man could
hate it. When the Lord was dishing out brains,
He must have sort of overlooked Butts."

Dora laughed. "When you first came to the
ranch I used to think that maybe He had overlooked you, too, Bruce," she said; "but I know
now that He didn't."

"Thanks," said Marvel.

At the head of the little party, trailing at comfortable distances through the hills, rode Cory
Blaine and Kay White. The man had been unusually quiet, even taciturn; but the girl, alert
and eager for each new beauty of this unaccus-
tomed trail, was glad for the long silences.

Sometimes her thoughts reverted to the harrowing incident of yesterday's lion hunt. Annoyingly persistent was the memory of a strong arm about her and of her own arms about a man's neck. The recollection induced no thrills, perhaps, but it had aroused a lively consciousness of the man that she had not felt before. It reminded her of the strength and courage and resourcefulness that his act had revealed, transforming him from a soon-to-be-forgotten incident in her life to a position of importance, where he would doubtless remain enshrined in her memory always. She had never given him much consideration. He had been agreeable in a self-effacing sort of way, and he was undeniably good-looking; but until yesterday he had never greatly aroused her interest.

We have all had similar experiences with chance acquaintances who were but additional names in the chaotic files of memory until some accident, perhaps trivial, precipitated them into the current of our lives, never to be entirely lost sight of or forgotten again, or perhaps to influence or direct our courses through rough or tranquil waters.

Her reveries were interrupted when Cory Blaine finally broke his long silence. "I can't help thinking," he said.

She waited for him to continue, but he did not. "Thinking what?" she asked.

"Thinking that everything is wrong. A fellow starts wrong and then he never gets the right break."

"What in the world are you talking about?"

"I never saw a girl like you before," he continued, "and now that I have found you, it is too late. I am what I am, and a fellow can't change in a minute. I might grow to be more like your kind, but that would take too long."

"You are all right as you are," she said.

"No, I'm not. If I was, you might love me as I love you."

"That has nothing to do with it," she said. "Love is unreasoning. It is purely instinctive. People are attracted to one another in that way or they are not. Haven't you often wondered lots of times what some married people saw in their mates that would have caused them to select the one they did above all others in the world?"

"I've wondered that about nearly all of them,"

Basalt Regional Library
P. O. Box BB
Basalt, Colo. 81621

admitted Blaine, "especially Benson Talbot; and that offers me some encouragement. One of them must have been attracted to the other first, like I am attracted to you; and then in some way the other one was won over. Don't you suppose, Kay, that I might win you?"

She shook her head. "No, Cory," she said. "I do not love you and that is all there is to it. Please don't talk about it anymore. It can only make us both unhappy."

"All right," he said, "I won't talk about it;" and then under his breath he muttered, "But by God, I'm going to have you."

They stopped presently in a grove of trees beside a mountain stream to rest and water their horses. Some of them had brought sandwiches; and when these were eaten, they mounted and rode on again; but this time Kay rode beside Bruce Marvel, and it was evident to Cory Blaine that the girl had arranged it so deliberately. He found himself paired off now with Birdie Talbot; and, being a good business man, he sought to be agreeable, though in his heart he had suddenly conceived an intense loathing for her, from her high heeled shoes to her ill-fitted sombrero.

viii

FOURFLUSHERS, ALL

KAY WHITE, on the other hand, found relief in her escape from Blaine's society, which, with the avowal of his love, she had found depressing and embarrassing. Marvel was companionable in that he was silent when she did not wish to talk; or equally willing to uphold his end of the conversation when she felt in the mood for it, though even then the brunt of it fell upon her, to which, being a woman, she was, naturally, not averse.

101

They had spoken casually of various things of interest along the trail and there had been long silences. It spoke well for the companionship of both of them that no matter how long these silences they never became strained; and then their conversation wandered to their horses, as conversations between horse lovers always do.

"I can't understand why Lightfoot behaved as he did yesterday," she said, speaking of her own mount.

"Most any horse loses his head easy," he said. "They are not like mules or cows. A mule isn't so nervous. If they get tangled up in something they usually lie still and wait for somebody to untangle them; but a horse will either kick himself free or to death, and he doesn't seem to care much which it is. Of course, they are not all alike. I saw an old horse once that had stood all night with one foot caught in a wire fence, and he hadn't moved. He just stood there till I happened along the next morning with a pair of pliers and cut him loose. He was a right old horse, and he must have got wise with age."

"Maybe if Lightfoot lives long enough he will have as much sense as a mule," suggested Kay.

"Maybe," he replied, "and then again maybe he won't. There are a lot of things, horses and men, too, who would never have any sense if they lived to be a thousand years old."

"He must have been terribly frightened yesterday," said the girl, "because he is always so sweet and gentle. Don't you suppose he would have stopped before the trail dropped off into the ravine?"

He shook his head. "I don't know," he said. "You can't always tell what a horse will do. Some folks say they're blind when they're frightened like that. I've seen them run right into a rail fence when they were real frightened, without even trying to jump it."

"It makes me shiver every time I think what might have happened if it hadn't been for you," she said.

He glanced up at her quickly. "It makes me feel mighty shaky, too," he said. "I am sure glad I was there."

"And you were the only one who thought to do it," she said.

"I reckon they knew their horses weren't fast enough," he said. "You know I knew Baldy could run. I've seen him run every morning; and he's built for speed, too. Anybody could see that. If I hadn't been sure he could beat Lightfoot, it would have been worse than useless to chase him, for then nothing on earth could have stopped him; and if you had jumped, the other horse might have hurt you."

"Every time I think of what you did I feel so ashamed of myself," said the girl.

"What have you got to be ashamed of?" he asked.

"I did you such an injustice," she said.

"You never did anything to me," he replied good naturedly.

"I mean in my thoughts," she explained. "I — it is rather hard to tell you, but I should feel like a hypocrite if I didn't."

"You don't have to," he said. "I think I know."

"I was deceived by outward appearances," she said.

"These clothes are sort of silly," he said; "I realize that now. Of course, though, when you are a stranger in a country it is hard to tell what to wear. You solved it though by adopting a sort of international garb. I guess overalls are worn everywhere."

"At least they are practical," she said, "and I am comfortable in them. It always seemed silly to me to dress up like an actor playing a part, especially when the part is one with which you are not familiar. Hikers who have never hiked, fliers who have never flown, golfers who have never golfed, and riders who have never ridden raid the sport tog shops seeking the last word in equipment and sartorial elegance, no matter how uncomfortable or weird the result. I remember hearing my father telling how he and mother fixed up when they got their first automobile — linen dusters, gauntlets, and goggles; and mama wore a veil with streaming ends that floated out in the wind behind the car. Now they haven't a single thing specially for motoring."

"I remember reading a little while ago about some chap who was after some trans-continental non-stop record, who had a special sky-blue uniform made, while Lindbergh was apt to cop off a record any afternoon in a business suit. No, you can't tell much about people by their clothes."

"Sometimes people try to deceive through the clothes that they wear," she remarked.

"Do you think that is wrong?" he asked.

"It depends upon what their purpose is, I suppose."

"Now Mrs. Talbot has the right idea," he said with a trace of a smile. "She aint trying to deceive anyone. She's dressed for hiking, golfing, riding or bridge. You can just take your choice, and I reckon that underneath she's got on a bathing suit."

"That's mean," she said.

"Oh, no, it aint mean," he defended himself. "Everybody has been making fun of me as though I was the only funny looking thing around, but perhaps I'm the only one that is dressed sensible and according to what he really is."

"Don't try to tell me that you are an Eastern polo player, Bruce," she said.

"I haven't," he said.

"But your clothes have tried to tell that," she insisted.

"But Dora's clothes just rear up on their hind legs and shout that she's a cowgirl, when she aint; and I'm sure I wouldn't be any funnier playing polo than you would be working in a section gang."

"I guess you're right," she said, laughing. "We are all of us fourflushers."

"Except Bud, perhaps," he suggested.

"How about Cory and Butts?" she asked. "How do you think they ought to be dressed?"

"If I told you you'd be surprised," he replied.

" 'All the world's a stage, and all the men and women merely players,' " she quoted.

" 'And one man in his time plays many parts,' " he added; "but a lot of us are bum actors."

"You are an enigma," she said.

"Why?" he asked.

She shook her head and did not reply. His recognition of her quotation from Shakespeare baffled her, for she had noted the carelessness of his English and his many lapses into Western vernacular; and, like Dora Crowell, with whom she had discussed him, she had come to the conclusion that he was a Westerner playing a part. It was Dora's theory that he had suddenly made a lot of money in Texas or Oklahoma oil and that, prompted by silly vanity, he was trying to pretend to be something that he was not. The more she saw of him and the longer she talked with him, the more convinced she became, however, that he was genuine at heart; and before they rode into camp that night she would have had to have admitted, had she asked herself the question, that she had found Marvel tremendously congenial and that she was more than a little interested in him.

Nor was she alone the troubled victim of an awakened interest. Perhaps a consciousness of the girl's personality had been developing within Marvel during the several days that he had known her, but it had not been until this afternoon that it had made itself objectively felt by him. It came suddenly, like an awakening, and with it a realization that this girl, a type such as he had never before met, had achieved a place in his thoughts that he had believed reserved forever for another.

The man's loyalty was inherent and almost entirely apart from any objective mental processes, so that the realization of his interest in Kay came at first in the nature of a distinct shock. He tried to put her out of his mind by conjuring the

features of the girl to whom he believed he owed
all the loyalty of his heart and mind; but if the
features of the absent one faded easily to be replaced by those of a little blonde in blue overalls,
it was not entirely surprising, for the one was
close and very real, while the other he had not
seen for years.

When she had gone away there had been no
understanding, only in his own heart; but to that
understanding he had always been loyal, and
upon it had been built a secret dream castle of
hope and longing.

Some day she would come back and he would
claim her, or, if she did not, he would go after
her wherever she might be; and so it was when
he looked at Kay and thoughts that he could not
govern came into his mind, he felt a distinct sense
of disloyalty to the other; and then Fate stepped
in and upset the applecart, for she caused him
to recall the moment that the girl had clung to
him with both arms about his neck. He felt
again the soft, lithe body pressed against his own;
and in that instant he was lost. But he tried not
to admit it even to himself; and inwardly he
swore that he would never speak of it to her, or,

at least, until he had laid his heart at the feet of the other girl. If she would not have it; then he could take it to Kay White with a clear conscience. But these were only dreams. When he brought his reason to bear upon the subject, he smiled cynically for he knew that there was little likelihood that Kay White would want his heart after he had brought it to her.

"A guy sure looks funny," he thought, "running around with his heart in his hand, offering it to different girls. That's what comes of reading poetry, I guess."

As the party sat around the fire that night after supper spinning yarns and discussing the events of the trip, it was noticeable that Cory Blaine had lost some of the suave and courteous manner of the host, and that he was especially short and almost disagreeable in the few remarks he was forced to address to Marvel.

The latter expressed his liking for Baldy. "Want to sell him, Blaine?" he asked.

"No," replied Cory shortly.

"I've taken a sort of fancy to him," said Bruce. "I'll give you more than he's worth."

"He wouldn't be much good to you," said

Butts, "unless you hired me to go along and top him for you every morning."

"Maybe I could learn to ride him," said Bruce. "I've learned lots of things since I've been up here. I'll give you seventy-five dollars for him, Blaine; and he aint worth over fifty, with the way the cattle business is today."

"What do you know about the cattle business?" demanded Blaine.

"Just what I hear," replied Marvel, "and since I've been out here I aint heard anything very good about it."

"That Baldy horse is worth a hundred dollars if he's worth a cent," said Cory, his avarice getting the better of his ill temper.

Marvel reached in his pocket and drew out a roll of bills. He handed Blaine five twenties. "Here you are," he said.

Blaine hesitated a moment and then reached out and took the money. "Baldy's yourn," he said.

As Bruce returned the roll of bills to his pocket, he commenced a hurried search of all the pockets in his clothes.

"Lost something?" asked Bud.

"Yes, I can't find my lucky tooth. I thought I had it this morning."

"Lucky tooth?" asked Dora.

"Sure," said Bruce. "Horse's tooth—better than a rabbit's foot."

"I never heard of such a thing," said Birdie Talbot.

"Live and learn," Marvel told her. "Now I'll have to find another one. Wouldn't do without a horse's tooth for anything."

One by one the members of the party rose and sought their blankets until only Kay White and Bruce Marvel were left sitting gazing into the glowing embers of the cook fire; but neither one felt the silence, and so they sat for some time until Kay finally roused herself and rose. "We both better go to bed," she said; "we have a long, hard ride tomorrow."

"Yes," he said, rising.

As she turned to go she paused. "Why did you buy Baldy?" she asked.

"He saved your life," he said simply.

She stood looking at him for a moment, the firelight playing on her golden hair and upon his bronzed face. Then she turned and walked away into the darkness, making no comment.

Marvel lit a cigarette, strolled over to the chuck wagon and picked up his bedroll; then he walked over and put it down close to where Cory Blaine lay.

After he had unrolled it, he went back to the fire and threw some more wood upon it before he removed his boots and crawled into his blankets.

Silence had fallen upon the camp, a silence broken only by the heavy breathing of some of the sleepers and the distant yapping of a coyote.

A half hour passed. The fire was still burning merrily. Bruce Marvel rose upon one elbow and listened attentively. Slowly he sat up and looked about the camp; then he reached over and picked up one of Cory Blaine's boots, where it lay under the edge of the sleeper's blankets. Taking careful and deliberate aim, he threw the boot into the fire; then he shouted loudly, "Get out of here, you!" whereupon Blaine and the other men awoke and sat up on their blankets.

"What's eatin' you?" demanded Blaine.

"There was a coyote sneaking around right in camp here," said Marvel, "and I threw my boot at him."

Blaine grunted and lay down again; and once more quiet reigned over the sleeping camp, and the smell of burning leather rose upward from the dying camp fire.

ix

The Sorrel Colt

Before dawn broke the cook was astir, growling and grumbling among his pots and kettles;
and then Cory Blaine awoke and reached for his
boots, but he found only one. He looked about
the camp in all directions and then he reached
over and shook Marvel by the shoulder. "Say,"
he demanded, as the sleeper awoke, "who the
hell's boot did you throw at that coyote?"

Marvel sat up and turned back the edge of his
bed, revealing a pair of natty English riding

boots. "By golly, Blaine," he exclaimed, "I'm awfully sorry. I must have thrown one of yours by mistake. I'll get into mine and go out and find it for you."

"It's funny how you could get hold of mine instead of your own," grumbled Cory.

"Isn't it?" agreed Marvel.

After Bruce had pulled on his boots he searched the camp, but no boot could he find. He questioned the cook and the cook helped him in the search, but all to no avail. Then Cory Blaine joined them with one foot bootless.

"The son-of-a-gun must have grabbed it and run off with it," suggested the cook.

"I sure am sorry," said Marvel.

Blaine mumbled something about damn fool tenderfeet and hobbled back to roll up his bed.

At breakfast Cory and Bruce were the objects of a great deal of good-natured raillery, which the former seemed to have considerable difficulty in appreciating.

"I'd loan you one of my boots," said Bruce, "but I'm afraid it wouldn't fit you."

"I wouldn't be buried in one of them things," replied Blaine surlily.

Kay White did not enter into the joking. She was very quiet and often she watched Bruce Marvel, as though she were studying him.

When it came time to mount, Marvel stood holding Baldy by the neck rope.

"Are you going to top him for me, Butts?" he asked.

"No," growled Butts, "I aint got time."

Marvel turned to Bud. "How about you, Bud?" he asked.

Bud grinned. "Aw, you can ride him all right," he said. "Anyway, we aint had no fun for a long while."

"I don't like to ask Cory to top him," said Bruce, "because he's only got one boot."

"Why don't you ask some of the ladies," suggested Butts. "Like as not, they aint afraid."

"Well, I guess I'll have to try it myself then," said Marvel.

"What sort of flowers do you want?" demanded Butts.

Bruce coiled the halter rope and gathered the reins in his left hand. He spoke in a low voice to Baldy and stroked his neck; then he swung easily into the saddle. Baldy did nothing. It was a great disappointment to everyone, except Marvel.

"What's the matter with him?" demanded Benson Talbot in an aggrieved tone.

"I don't think you're a bit nice," said Dora Crowell to Marvel. "You might have got thrown once, at least."

"Sorry to disappoint you," said Bruce. "I'll fall off him, anyway, if you say so."

"I wish you would," muttered Blaine under his breath, "and break your fool neck."

As they started out Kay rode beside Bruce. He tried to engage the girl in conversation, but soon saw that she did not care to talk and desisted; nor was it until the party had stretched out along the trail and the two were alone that she broke her silence.

"After I got to my tent last night, I did not feel like sleeping," she said; "and so I went out a little way from camp and sat on a rock that I had noticed there before dark. In front of me was the camp, illuminated by the camp fire. Behind me lay the hills, mysterious under the starlight. I saw you pick something up and throw it into the fire. Until this morning I did

not know what it was.   I heard you yell at something, as though to chase it away; but there was
nothing there.   I was so surprised last night that
I just sat there until the camp had quieted down
again before I returned to my tent.   I cannot
imagine why you did it, but I want to tell you
that I think it was a small and petty thing to do.
I should think that you would be ashamed of
yourself.   Even if you were a little child, playing a joke, it would still be detestable."   Her
voice was low, but her tone touched like ice.   He
could see that she was thoroughly disgusted.

"I am sorry that you saw it."   That was all he
said.

The party had gotten an early start that morning with the intention of riding all the way
through to the ranch, leaving the chuck wagon,
which they no longer needed, to trail along in at
its own gait; so that the same trip that had required three days going up into the mountains
required only two coming out.

The hunters arrived at the home camp in the
middle of the afternoon; and after greeting those
who had been left behind, each repaired to his
room to clean up and to read his mail.

Bruce Marvel had none; so he was soon out again, wandering about the ranch yard. Presently Blaine emerged from his quarters and walked down toward the corral. He had donned a pair of old and well worn boots — boots that had once been resplendent with patent leather designs in two colors embellishing their tops and with little brass hearts set in the center of each heel.

As Bruce Marvel followed Cory Blaine into the dusty corral, his eyes were on the ground and he appeared to be absorbed in deep meditation; yet he was humming a gay little tune, an occupation which was so much at variance with his accustomed quiet that it elicited a comment from Blaine. "What's ticklin' you?" he demanded. "Get a letter from your gal?"

"No," said Marvel, "I haven't got any gal; but I just got some good news."

Blaine made no comment, but he had stopped as though he had something more to say to Marvel; however, it was the latter who spoke first. "Can you rent me a fresh horse, Blaine?" he asked.

"What do you want with a horse?" demanded

the superintendent. "You've been ridin' all day."

"I just want to ride around a bit and see if I can find me another horse's tooth," explained Bruce. "There must be plenty of old skulls around here somewhere."

"Sure they is," said Blaine, "if you can find them."

"I can try," said Marvel. "I don't feel safe without a horse's tooth — greatest luck charm in the world."

"I aint got no very gentle horse up now," explained Blaine. "They are all out in pasture, and it might take a half an hour to get 'em up."

"What have you got?" asked Bruce.

"Nuthin' but an old crowbait that we use for wranglin' and a colt one of the boys is bustin'."

"That sorrel there?" asked Marvel, indicating a horse standing in a stall in the stable.

"Yes."

"I saw one of the boys riding him before we went on the lion hunt," said Marvel. "He didn't seem very wild."

"You can take him if you want, but if you have to walk home don't blame me none."

"I'm not going far anyway," said Marvel; "so it won't be a long walk."

"Just as you say," said Blaine. "I'll saddle him for you."

He led the animal out of the stable, and Marvel held him while the other man saddled and bridled him.

"I'll take him outside of the corral," said Blaine. "You'd better mount him out there where there's lots of room. You may need it."

Marvel stroked the colt's neck and spoke to him as he had with Baldy; then he eased himself into the saddle, slowly and gently, and started off down the road at a walk.

Blaine stood watching him, his brows knitted as the horse and rider grew smaller and smaller in the distance. They were almost out of sight when Blaine straightened up expectantly — the colt had commenced to pitch.

Blaine grinned. "I guess that damn dude will walk home all right," he muttered.

The sorrel was pitching and he was pitching hard. Even from a distance, the watcher could see that; and he could see that he was bringing into play every broncho artifice for unseating his rider short of throwing himself to the ground.

Gradually the smile faded from Blaine's lips, and there crept into his eyes an expression of astonishment not unmixed with trouble. "The son-of-a-gun," he muttered, or something that sounded like that; but whether he referred to the horse or the rider, one may not definitely know.

Perhaps the sorrel pitched for four or five minutes — it seemed like fifteen to Cory Blaine — and then the rider evidently got the animal's head up and the two disappeared around the shoulder of a hill, the horse moving at an easy lope.

"The son-of-a-gun!" repeated Cory Blaine; and then, "I never did like that hombre anyway."

Bruce Marvel rode hard and fast, and he did not appear to be looking for horses' teeth along the way. The sun was setting when he rode into the railroad town at which, scarcely a week before, he had left the train and taken the buckboard for the ranch.

He tied his horse to the rail before the general store in which the postoffice was located; and after purchasing some stationery and a postage stamp, he wrote a brief letter, sealed and ad-

dressed the envelope, and dropped it into the slot
for outgoing mail.

That he was the object of the amused interest
of the few people whom he encountered in the
store and on the street did not appear to concern
him at all; and after watering the sorrel and readjusting the blanket and cinches, he mounted
and started back through the growing dusk toward the ranch, where the guests were already
sitting down to supper.

"Where is Bruce?" asked Dora Crowell,
when, the meal half over, he had not appeared.

"He went out hunting horses' teeth," said
Blaine. "I reckon he didn't have much luck."

"Who ever heard of a horse's tooth bringing
good luck?" demanded Birdie Talbot.

"No one," said her husband.

"I think he's crazy," said Birdie.

"Oh, he seemed a very nice young man," said
Miss Pruell.

"Birdie thinks anyone's crazy who doesn't play
bridge with her," said Benson.

"Nothing of the sort," snapped Birdie. "I
just think they're a little peculiar."

"Do you remember the English lord, Birdie,

who made such a wonderful bridge partner at Fishkill-on-the-Hudson that summer?"

"That might have happened to anyone," snapped Mrs. Talbot.

"Birdie was always quoting him as an authority on bridge and everything else until they came and took him away. He had escaped from Matteawan."

"And wasn't he an English lord at all?" asked Miss Pruell.

"No," said Talbot, "he had been a school teacher in Poughkeepsie until the night he killed his wife for trumping his ace."

Experience had taught Cory Blaine that his Eastern guests especially enjoyed the stories and the rough humor of the cowhands, and so it was customary for some of the men to stroll up to the house during the evening and join the group upon the wide veranda.

X

BLAINE IS JEALOUS

TONIGHT THEY were later than usual in coming, and only Bud and Butts put in an appearance.

"Where's the dude with the panties?" inquired Bud, noting Marvel's absence.

"He is out looking for a horse's tooth," explained Dora.

"The poor nut," said Butts disgustedly, "hoofin' it around at night looking for a horse's tooth."

"He is not on foot and he started out in the daytime," said Kay White. "Don't you think someone ought to go out and look for him, Cory?"

"What's he ridin'?" asked Bud.

"The sorrel colt," said Blaine.

Butts whistled. "Sure we better go out and look for him," he said, "and we better take a basket or some blotting paper."

"Why?" asked Kay.

"That there sorrel's probably killed the dude by this time and spread him all over the landscape," explained Butts. "He sure is some ornery bronc."

"Oh, Cory, you shouldn't have let him take a bad horse like that," said Kay.

"I warned him," said Blaine, "but he wanted to take the horse anyway."

"You sure better send out a search party, Cory," said Butts. "That colt has the makin's of a good horse in him. It would be too bad to lose him."

"Here comes someone now," exclaimed Dora Crowell; and as all eyes turned in the direction of the road they saw a horseman approaching.

He rode up to the veranda. "Is Butts here?" he asked, and they recognized the voice as Marvel's.

"Yea," said Butts. "What do you want?"

Marvel dismounted. "Take my horse, my man," he said.

If there is anything that will wreck a cowman's equanimity it is to be treated like a menial; and no carefully studied insult would have been more effective than the use of "my man" in addressing the puncher; but Cory Blaine, who was sitting next to Butts, nudged him with his elbow before the man could make an angry reply; and Butts arose, boiling with rage, and taking the reins from Marvel led the colt away toward the stables.

"Where you been so long?" asked Blaine.

"I guess I must have got lost," exclaimed Marvel.

"Did you have any trouble with the colt?" asked Bud.

"Not a bit," said Marvel. "He was just like a kitten."

"Didn't he pitch at all?" asked Blaine.

"Not a pitch," replied Marvel.

"And you didn't find a horse's tooth?" asked Birdie.

"No," replied Marvel, "I didn't; but I'm going to get Bud to take me down tomorrow to where he knows there is a dead horse. Will you do that, Bud?"

"What dead horse?" demanded Blaine.

"I heard somebody say something about a horse dropping dead here a few weeks ago," explained Bruce.

"Sure I'll take you down tomorrow," said Bud.

"You must be hungry," said Kay. "You haven't had any supper, have you?"

"It won't hurt me any to miss a meal," said Bruce.

"Come on, I'll get you a sandwich," said Kay. "I guess the cook won't murder me." She arose and led the way into the kitchen.

"This is mighty good of you, Kay," said Marvel; "but I didn't want to put anyone to any trouble. I should not have been late."

The darkness hid the scowl upon Blaine's face. He muttered something under his breath.

"What was that, Cory?" asked Dora.

"There's something fishy about that bozo,"

said Blaine, recalling Marvel's statement that the colt had not pitched with him.

"Oh, any tenderfoot might get lost here after dark," contended the girl.

"Tenderfoot, my hat!" mumbled Blaine.

"The colt would have come back by himself, if he'd given him his head," said Bud. "He's raised right here on the ranch."

By the time Kay and Bruce had returned from the kitchen, Butts had come back from the stables. "You must have rid that horse pretty hard, Mister," he said to Marvel.

"Must I?" inquired Bruce.

"That's what I said, Mister," snapped Butts in an ugly tone.

"I heard you, my man," replied Marvel. "I aint deaf."

Butts started to rise. It was evident to him, as it was to some of the others, that Marvel was deliberately baiting him. His voice had been soft and low, but he had put just the right inflection on certain words to raise them to the dignity of insults.

Blaine laid a hand upon Butts' leg. "Sit down," he said in a low voice.

"I aint goin' to let no ——"

"Sit down," said Blaine sharply, "and shut up." And Butts did as he was bid.

"What's new?" asked Marvel. "It seems almost like I've been gone a week."

"I got a letter from my father," said Kay. "He may be along here any day."

"Is that so," said Bruce. "Well that surely is nice."

"When did he say he'd get here?" asked Cory.

"He didn't say exactly; in fact, he didn't know when he could start; but from what he did write I imagine that he may be here any time now."

"Well, he'd wire you, wouldn't he?" asked Blaine; "so that we could meet the train."

"He is not coming by train," replied Kay. "He's driving on."

"Oh," said Blaine; and then, "When was the letter dated?"

"About four days ago. You see it came while we were on the lion hunt."

"How long would it take him to drive here?" persisted Cory.

"He likes to take it easy; so I imagine it would take him three or four days."

"Oh, by the way," exclaimed Dora Crowell, "there's a friend of mine coming up, Cory. I want you to save a room for her."

"When is she coming?" asked Blaine.

"Well, I don't know that, either. She said she would come just as soon as she could get away. It's Olga Gunderstrom, you know. You heard me speak of her before. She said she had a few more matters to settle up; and then she could get away for a week or ten days, and she wants to come up here with me and rest. I imagine it has been pretty hard for her."

"The poor child," said Miss Pruell sympathetically.

"Did she say whether they found the murderer yet or not?" asked Cory.

"No, but they are pretty sure now that it was Buck Mason. They can't find trace of him anywhere."

"Is that the only reason they got for suspecting him?" asked Marvel.

"What more reason do you want?" asked Butts. "Who else could it have been?"

"Well, maybe you're right," said Marvel; "but that's sort of slim evidence to hang a man on."

"They have more than that," said Dora.

"Oh, have they?" asked Marvel.

"An Indian turned up two or three weeks after the murder who said that he saw Buck Mason riding away from Mr. Gunderstrom's cabin late in the afternoon of the murder."

"I guess they got that guy hogtied all right," said Butts.

"It certainly looks like it," agreed Marvel.

"There aint no doubt but what he done it," said Butts.

"They are trying to find the man who telephoned the sheriff's office and gave the clew," said Dora. "They can't imagine who it could have been; but now they are commencing to think that Mason was one of the gang that has been robbing banks and paymasters all around there for the last year, and that one of his own men, who had it in for him, tipped off the sheriff."

"That certainly sounds like a good theory," said Marvel, "but how are they going to find the fellow that called up?"

"That's where the trouble comes in," said Dora. "Olga wrote me that the only clew that they have to him is that an old man by the name of Cage, who received the message, said that the man talked as though he had a harelip."

"That's not much of a clew," said Blaine. "There's a lot of men in the country with harelips."

"Well, if they're going to hang all the men with harelips and all the men that haven't been seen around Comanche County for the last three or four weeks, they've got some wholesale job cut out for themselves," said Bruce with a laugh. "When did you say Miss Gunderstrom was coming, Dora?"

"I may get a telegram most any time," replied Dora.

"I'll save a room for her," said Blaine. "I'm expecting a party of four or five on from Detroit, but we'll make room some way for Kay's father and Miss Gunderstrom."

Birdie Talbot suppressed a yawn. "My gracious," she said, "I'm nearly dead. I think we should all go to bed."

"That's the first really bright remark anyone has made this evening," said Dora.

The suggestion seemed to meet with general approval; and as the guests rose to go to their rooms, Cory motioned to Marvel. "I want to see you a minute," he said. "See you fellows in the morning," he said to Butts and Bud; and then when the two were alone, he turned back to Marvel. "How much longer you figurin' on bein' here?" he asked.

"I like it first rate here," replied Marvel. "I was planning on staying awhile."

"Well, I got all these people comin' now," said Blaine, "and I'll be needin' your room pronto."

"When do you expect the people from Detroit?" asked Marvel.

"They may be along any day now," replied Blaine.

"Then I'll wait 'till they come," said Marvel; and turning, he entered the house.

"Wait," said Blaine, "there's one more thing."

Marvel turned in the doorway. "What is it?" he asked.

"I'm sort of responsible for these girls here," said Blaine. "I got to look after 'em. It's just hands off, do you understand?"

"I hear, but I don't understand," replied Marvel.

"If you know what's good for your health, you will understand," snapped Cory.

For a moment the two men stood looking at each other, and the air was charged with hostility. Then Blaine walked down the porch to the entrance to his own room, and Bruce Marvel disappeared within the interior of the ranch house.

"So," thought Marvel, as he entered his room and lighted his oil lamp, "Mr. Blaine is jealous. I'm glad that it isn't anything else. He sure had me guessing though at first."

After he had taken off his outer clothing, Marvel opened his trunk and extracted a suit of silk pajamas. They were brand new and had never been worn. He examined them critically as he had upon several other similar occasions and then he replaced them carefully in the trunk and slipped into bed in his underclothing. "I suppose I'll have to learn to wear 'em some day," he murmured; "but, Lord, what if the house would get on fire when a fellow was wearing things like that?" And he was still shuddering at the thought as he fell asleep, to dream of a blonde head and blue denim overalls.

Late that night a fire burned upon the summit of a rocky hill below the ranch house, but none of the sleeping inmates saw it, and by morning it was only cold ashes.

XI

"THAT WOULD BE EDDIE"

BRUCE MARVEL was a few minutes late for breakfast the following morning, and all of the guests were seated when he entered the dining room. He greeted them with the quiet smile with which they had become so familiar, and a casual word here and there in reply to the banal remarks to the accompaniment of which a group of human beings usually starts the day. Cory Blaine alone did not look up as he entered, a fact which did not seem to abash Marvel in the least.

"Good morning, Cory," he said cheerily.

"Mornin'," grumbled Blaine.

"Ready for the paper chase, Bruce?" asked Kay White.

"What paper chase?" he asked.

"Oh, that's so, you weren't at supper last night, were you?" continued the girl. "We arranged it all then. We are going to have a paper chase today."

"I'm sorry," spoke up Cory, "but I can't go today. I've got to attend to a little business, and I figured on letting Bud take you all over to Crater Mountain. There aint any of you seen that, and it's worth seein'. Tomorrow we'll have the paper chase."

"One day is as good as another," said the girl, "and I've always wanted to see the crater of the old volcano."

"Pshaw!" exclaimed Marvel. "I was figurin' that Bud could help me find a horse's tooth this morning."

Blaine looked up at him in disgust and then suddenly the light of inspiration shone in his eyes. "Why that can be fixed up all right," he said good-naturedly. "Butts can just as well take the folks over to Crater Mountain, and you and Bud can go tooth huntin'."

"Oh, that's mean," said Dora; "why don't you come along with us?"

"Maybe I'll find the tooth and catch up with you," he said; but his thoughts were not upon his words; instead they were occupied with the wish that Kay White had said that instead of Dora Crowell.

After breakfast they all went to the corral while the men caught up the horses for the day. There was the usual rush and movement and excitement that seems never to pall even upon those most accustomed to seeing it. The cleverness of the horses and the cleverness of the men, the kaleidoscopic changes of form and color, the smell of horses, the clashing hoofs, the dust of the corral all combine to produce a spell that lingers forever in the memory.

Blaine was issuing instructions to his men, selecting for the riders horses that had been left at home during the lion hunt.

"I think I'll ride Baldy," said Marvel. "I won't be doing much today."

"Suit yourself," said Blaine. "Bud, you're

going with Mr. Marvel hunting teeth. Butts will take the folks over to Crater Mountain."

"You better pack along a thirty-thirty," said Butts to Bud. "Some of them teeth is pretty wild. I knew a tenderfoot once who come out from the East huntin' teeth. He went out alone without a gun and he got bit all up."

It being customary to laugh at such witticisms, everyone now laughed, including Marvel, who stood speculatingly scrutinizing Butts' bowed legs. "I wish Butts was going with me instead of Bud," he said.

"Why?" demanded Butts. "I aint no wet nurse."

"But you're just what a fellow needs when he's hunting teeth," insisted Marvel.

"How do you make that out?" asked Butts.

"Well, you see, I'd take along a gunny sack and stretch it between your legs and chase the teeth in."

"Well I won't be along," said Butts; "so you better shoot 'em; but be sure to aim at somethin' else or you won't never hit 'em."

"I guess that'll hold you, Bruce," said Dora.

"I guess it ought to," he said grinning.

A moment later, as Kay White's horse was led out of the corral, Marvel stepped over as she was about to mount and examined the bridle, the bit, and the cinches.

"I'm sorry you are not going today," she said in a low voice.

"Are you really?" he asked.

She nodded. "But I suppose there is nothing so important as a horse's tooth."

He looked at her and smiled. "It means a lot to me, Kay," he said. "Anything would have to mean a lot to keep me from riding to Crater Mountain today."

There was something in his tone that checked whatever reply she might have made, and in silence she mounted as he held her horse; and then the others rode up around them and carried her along, but he watched her for a long time as she rode away toward the hills to the East.

"Here's your horse, Mister," called Blaine from the corral, interrupting Marvel's reverie. "Want me to top him for you?"

"Oh, I don't think he'll do anything."

"He certainly won't do anything more than the sorrel colt," said Blaine.

"Well he didn't do nothing; so I guess I'm safe," said Bruce.

As Marvel and Bud rode away down the valley, Blaine stood looking after them. "I sure don't like that bozo," he said aloud. "I just aint got no time for him; but," after a pause, "I'll be damned if I know why."

Marvel and Bud rode side by side at a slow walk. "We might have a look at that horse of Blaine's that fell dead a few weeks ago," suggested the former.

"I'm afraid it's pretty fresh," said Bud.

"We can have a look at it anyway," said Marvel. "Where is it?"

They rode down the valley for about a mile and well off the road when, suddenly, several vultures rose just ahead of them.

"There it be," said Bud.

They rode closer. "It is a bit fresh, isn't it?" asked Marvel. Between coyotes, vultures and rodents the horse had pretty well disappeared; but the stench was still overpowering, yet Marvel rode close up to the putrid remains.

He sat looking down at the grizzly thing for half a minute; then he turned and rode away.

"I guess it's a little bit too high even for me," he said.

"Well," said Bud, "there ought to be others. It seems to me I seen a horse's skull down the wash about a half a mile farther," but Marvel seemed suddenly to have lost interest in horse teeth.

"Oh, never mind, Bud," he said. "I guess I'll let it go till another day."

"That's funny," said Bud. "You sure was keen for it a little while ago."

He did not see the figure of a horseman winding into the hills in the West, and had he, he might not have connected it with the tenderfoot's sudden loss of interest in horse teeth; but Marvel had seen and he had recognized both horse and rider, even though they were little more than a speck against the hillside.

Marvel and Bud rode slowly toward the ranch. The former, riding slightly in the rear, was scrutinizing his companion meditatively.

"How long you been with this outfit, Bud?" asked Marvel presently.

"I've always been on the ranch. I was born there. My uncle used to own it. When Cory turned it into a boarding house I went to work for him."

"Known him long?"

"Couple of years."

"I don't see how he makes a living out of his boarders," said Bruce.

"It's been tough goin' until lately," replied Bud. "It's pickin' up now; but he always seems to have plenty of dough. He has a mine somewhere, he says, and a ranch, too."

"I guess he'd be needing them," said Bruce, "to keep up this outfit; but I don't see how he runs two or three businesses."

"Oh, he and Butts go away every once in a while to look after his other interests."

"You never went with him?" asked Marvel.

"No, he never took me along. He leaves me here to look after things while he's away."

As they talked, Marvel had dropped back until Baldy's head was about opposite Bud's knee. Riding in this position, Bud did not see his companion raise one of his feet and remove a spur, which he quietly slipped inside his shirt.

"I should think all these boarders would get on his nerves," said Bruce.

"Some of them do," replied Bud.

"Me, for instance," suggested Bruce. Bud grinned.

"Hell!" exclaimed Marvel, "I've lost a spur." He reined in and so did Bud.

"Let's go back and look for it," said Bud.

"No," replied Marvel, "you go on back to the ranch. I'll look for it myself."

"Pshaw!" exclaimed Bud. "I'd just as soon help you find it."

"No, you go on back to the ranch. I've learned what a nuisance a dude is, and I'll feel better if you just go on and let me find it for myself."

"Whatever you say," said Bud. "We aim to please, as the feller said."

"See you later," said Marvel; and reining Baldy about he started back down the valley.

At a point where a dry wash came out of the hills from the West he stopped and turned in his saddle. Bud was jogging quietly toward home, his back turned. For a few seconds Marvel watched him; then he headed into the dry wash, the high banks of which would hide him from Bud's view should the latter happen to turn his eyes backward.

Now he rode more swiftly, spurring Baldy into a lope, until the ascent toward the hills became too steep.

The arroyo he was following led to the summit of low hills near the point where he had seen the rider disappear shortly before; and as he neared the top he went more slowly, finally stopping just before he reached the ridge. Dismounting he dropped Baldy's reins to the ground and covered the remaining distance on foot.

It was a barren ridge, supporting but a scant growth of straggling brush. As he neared the top he dropped to his hands and knees and crawled the remaining distance to a point just behind a small bush that grew upon the crest of the ridge. Here he lay on his belly and wormed himself a few inches farther upward until his eyes topped the summit.

Beyond the ridge and below him lay a barren gully, in the bottom of which, a hundred yards up from the point at which he was spying on them, three men sat in their saddles; and one of them was addressing the other two rapidly and earnestly. This one was Cory Blaine.

An expression of satisfaction crossed Marvel's

face. "That," he said enigmatically, "will be the other two."

For ten minutes Marvel lay there watching the three men in the gully below. Then he saw them gather their reins. Blaine spurred his horse up the side of the gully, while the other two turned down toward the valley.

Half way up the hillside Blaine reined in his mount and turned in the saddle. "Don't you fellers do no drinking tonight," he shouted back at the two below him, "and see that you are there on time tomorrow."

"Sure, boss," shouted back one of them in a thick, almost inarticulate voice.

"And that what I said about drinking goes double for you, Eddie," called Blaine, as he turned his horse's head upward again toward the summit of the ridge.

Marvel returned to Baldy and mounted him. Then he urged the horse at a reckless pace down the rough wash. Near the mouth of the arroyo he reined to the left, urging Baldy up the steep bank and across a low ridge; then he put the spurs to him, and ignoring the rocky terrain and the menace of innumerable badgers' holes he cut downward across the rolling hills parallel with the valley at a run.

Where the ridge finally melted into the floor of the valley, he reined Baldy to the left and so came at last into the mouth of the barren gully in which he had seen the three men talking.

Riding toward him now were two of the men, and as he came into view they eyed him intently. With what appeared to be considerable effort, he stopped Baldy in front of them, while they reined in their own ponies and viewed him with ill-concealed contempt.

"Who let you out, sister?" demanded one of them.

Marvel looked embarrassed. "My horse ran away with me," he explained, "and I guess I'm lost."

"Where you lost from, sis?" demanded one of the riders with exaggerated solicitude, and in the scarcely articulate tone that Marvel had previously heard when the speaker had addressed Blaine.

"That," soliloquized he, "would be Eddie;" and then aloud, "I'm stopping at the TF Ranch. Could you direct me how to get there?"

"Certainly," said Eddie. "Go straight up this here gulch." Then the men moved on.

"Them directions," said the second man, "will land the son-of-a-gun in Mexico, if he follows them."

"Well, they aint got no business roamin' around Arizona without their nurses," replied Eddie.

Marvel watched the two for a moment, his keen eyes taking in every detail of both men and horses. Then he rode slowly up the gulch, following the trail that the two had made going up and coming down, his eyes often bent upon the ground. When he reached the point where Blaine had spurred up over the ridge, he did likewise and presently dropped down into the valley on the other side where the ranch lay; and as he rode into the ranch yard, Eddie, far away, was still chuckling over the joke he had played upon the tenderfoot.

Today, seeing no one about the corral, he removed the bridle and saddle himself and turned Baldy into the pasture.

As he approached the ranch house, Blaine and Bud emerged from the former's room, which was also his office.   "Find your spur?" asked Bud.

"Yes," replied Bruce.

"You must have had to chase it all over the county," said Blaine.   "Bud says he left you three hours ago."

"I guess I got lost again," explained Bruce.

"You dudes are a damn nuisance," snapped Cory, all his usual suavity gone.

Marvel raised his eyebrows.   "Our money aint such a nuisance, is it?" he asked.

"I got all your money I'm going to," said Blaine.   "You'll be leavin' now.   Them folks are comin' from Detroit right away."

"I'm about ready to leave anyway," replied Marvel, "but I think I'll stay until after the paper chase.   I certainly would like to be in on that."

"The paper chase needn't detain you none," snapped Blaine, "and I'll be wantin' your room tomorrow morning."

"What's the rush?" demanded Marvel. "Whenever those folks come they can have my room."

Whatever reply Blaine may have contemplated was interrupted by Bud.   "Here comes the bunch back from Crater Mountain," he announced; and he and Cory hurried down to the corral to meet them, followed more slowly by Marvel.

Conversation during dinner was occupied largely with the events of the day and plans for the paper chase on the morrow. Cory explained that he and Bud would be the hares, taking one other member of the party with him, whom he would select in the morning.

xii

"Goodbye, Kay"

THE GUESTS retired early that evening, with the exception of Marvel, who sat alone on the veranda smoking. Blaine and Butts were sitting on the top rail of the corral talking. "I'm gettin' rid of Marvel tomorrow," said Cory.

"What you so asceared of him for?" demanded Butts. "He's harmless."

"He's sweet on Kay White," replied Blaine. "I want her for myself."

"Well, aint you goin' to get her?"

"Yes, but I think she sort of likes the dude; and if he's around he may bust it up after I get it fixed."

"Now that he's goin'," said Butts, "I sure would like to make him dance."

"Nuthin' doin'," said Blaine. "Anything like that would give us a bad reputation."

"I sure would like to take a shot at that dude just the same," said Butts.

"Well, you aint goin' to," said Blaine. "He don't mean nuthin' to me except to get him out of the way of Kay White as easy as I can. See that you don't go mussin' things up."

"Just as you say, boss," replied Butts, "but my trigger finger sure itches every time I look at that son-of-a-gun."

On the ranch house veranda Marvel had stamped out the fire of his last cigarette and was sitting with his feet on the rail thinking.

"I guess," he meditated, "that it's just about as well that I get out of here anyway, for if I don't I'm going to fall in love with Kay White — if I haven't already fallen. Of course, I aint give no one else a promise except in my own heart, and I think she knew before she went away that I'd be

waiting for her when she came back.   It's a funny
world.   I wonder what she'll be like."

He was sitting in the shadows at the end of the
porch when a light step attracted his attention;
and looking down the long veranda he saw a slender figure emerge from the house, and as he saw
it a little thrill ran through his frame.

He did not speak nor move, fearing perhaps
that he might frighten her away.   She came
slowly along the veranda toward him, reveling
in the cool night air and the star-shot heaven
against which the black hills stood out in sharply
defined silhouette.   She was quite close before
she discovered him, and when she did she voiced
a little exclamation of surprise.

"I didn't know that there was anyone out here,"
she said; and, coming closer, "Oh, it's you."

"It's so much nicer out here," he said, "that I
hated to go into that stuffy little box."

"That's the way I felt.   I could not sleep."

"I am glad that you couldn't."

"That is not very nice," she said, smiling.

"You know what I mean," he said.   "Won't
you sit down?"   Rising, he drew another chair
closer to his own.

"I might for a minute," she said, "but —— "

"But you would rather be alone. I know how that is. Lots of times I feel that way myself, most of the time in fact; but I'll promise not to talk."

"I don't mind if you talk," she told him, "if you don't make me talk."

"Then I reckon it won't be very noisy out here."

She settled herself comfortably in her chair. "That will be nice. There are so few people who know when to keep still."

He smiled contentedly, but made no reply; and, having purposely arranged the chairs to this end, he sat admiring her profile and lazily permitted himself to indulge in thoughts that were not entirely loyal to another girl. It was a long silence that followed — a silence which the girl was first to break.

"Do you think the paper chase will be good sport?" she asked.

"I hope so," he said.

"Cory has promised that I can be one of the hares," she continued.

"Oh."

"Do you think you can catch us?"

"I am not going along," he said.

"Why?" she asked in surprise.

"I'm leaving tomorrow," he told her.

"Leaving!" she exclaimed, sitting erect and turning toward him. "Not leaving for good?"

"Yes."

"Oh, I am sorry. I thought perhaps that you would be here longer."

"Cory wants my room. He has other guests coming."

"Did he ask you to leave?"

"Yes, but I was about ready to go anyway."

"I don't see why he couldn't make room for you," she said. "Dora and I could double up, or you could go in with Bert Adams."

"I sort of guess Cory wouldn't thank anyone for the suggestion."

"You mean that he doesn't want you to stay? Why in the world shouldn't he?"

"Maybe I haven't paid my bill."

"I know better than that," she said. "You paid a week in advance when you came. I heard you and Cory talking about it, and I saw you pay him for Baldy; so I know that you can't owe him anything."

"I suppose he's got his own reasons," said Bruce.

"I don't see what they could be."

"Don't you?" he asked.

There was a curious inflection to the question that perhaps he did not intend, but she sensed a hidden meaning which piqued her curiosity. "Why should I?" she demanded.

"Oh, nothing," he said, moving uneasily in his chair.

"It is something," she insisted. "It sounds as though in some way I were responsible."

"Oh, you aint to blame. It's just that Cory has foolish ideas in his head, though perhaps they aint so foolish after all," he added.

"You have got to tell me," she said. "I certainly have a right to know if I have done anything."

"I told you you haven't done anything."

"Well, then, I want to know anyway," she said with finality.

"It's just that Cory thinks," he started, and then he gave a nervous cough and started over again. "It's just that Cory thinks — by golly, Kay, I can't say it."

She looked at him, her eyes wide; for he had told her everything in his halting speech and embarrassed manner, though doubtless he would have sworn that he had told her nothing.

She rose slowly from her chair and stood looking out into the night for a moment. Now she was moving away, along the veranda toward the doorway. "Good night," she said.

"Good-bye, Kay."

She did not reply as she moved rapidly toward her room.

He sat there alone and in silence until midnight, while Kay White tossed sleeplessly upon her bed. Here was another problem, and that it had suddenly become a serious one she recognized now that the man's unconscious avowal had brought a realization of the depth of her interest in him — an interest that had been constantly mounting since the day of the lion hunt.

She was glad that he was going away on the morrow and that she would never see him again, for something seemed to tell her that he might be a very difficult person to resist; and perhaps, too, she realized he might be almost as equally difficult to forget.

She kept congratulating herself over and over again that she had not fallen in love with him, and thus she fell asleep.

At breakfast the next morning, Bruce Marvel appeared in his street clothes, much to the surprise of every one, except Cory Blaine and Kay White.

"Why the smart togs?" demanded Dora Crowell. "Are they the last word in paper chase raiment?"

"I'm leaving today," he explained.

"Oh, I think that is real mean," said Birdie Talbot. "We haven't had a single game of bridge."

"We shall certainly be sorry to see you go, Mr. Marvel," said Miss Pruell.

"Well, we made a horseman of him, anyway, before he left," chimed in Bert Adams.

"I envy you, Bruce," said Benson Talbot; "I'd like to get back to God's country, where there's a golf course, myself."

"Butts is goin' down to the train to meet a party," announced Blaine. "He'll take you and your stuff along with him."

"What are you going to do with Baldy?" asked Dora.

"I'm going to take him along with me," replied Marvel.

"Want to sell him?" asked Adams. "I'll give you what you paid Cory for him."

"I'm not aimin' ever to sell Baldy," replied Marvel; and Kay White knew that the words were meant for her.

xiii

Marvel Buys an Outfit

After breakfast Bruce watched the party get away on the paper chase. He saw Cory and Kay and Bud start up the valley fifteen minutes ahead of the others. At the last minute the girl had come and given him her hand in parting. "Good bye, Bruce," she said. "I'm sorry that you are not going to be here when my father comes. He will be sorry not to have been able to thank you for what you did that day."

"I didn't do it for thanks, Kay," he said.

"They are taken for granted anyway.   Anyhow, Kay, he couldn't be any more thankful than I."

"Hurry up!" growled Blaine.   "If we want to get back tonight, we better get started."

Marvel pressed the girl's hand.   "Good bye, Kay," he said, and a moment later she was gone.

When the rest of the party had ridden away, Marvel and Butts found themselves alone at the corral.

The cowboy turned toward the city man. "We'll be leavin' right after dinner, Mister," he said.   "The train's due about three."

"I'll be ready," said Marvel, and turned back toward the house, where Miss Pruell was sitting on the veranda, her embroidery lying in her lap, her eyes strained up the valley following the dust of the riders.

Marvel joined her.   "Rather lonesome for you, Miss Pruell," he said.

"Oh, I don't mind it a bit," she replied, "only that I worry so much about Kay.   I shall be glad when her father gets here, because I don't like the idea of her riding off alone with strange men."

"Mrs. Talbot and Dora are along."

"But Kay and Cory and Bud started fifteen minutes ahead of the others, and I don't think it's proper at all. I just can't get used to the ways of modern young people, Mr. Marvel. I'm too old-fashioned, and I always shall be."

"I guess I'm a little bit old-fashioned myself, Miss Pruell. I would rather have seen one of the other ladies go along with Kay."

"Do you think there is any danger?" she asked, perturbed.

"Oh, my no," he assured her. "It is you and I probably who are wrong."

"Well, I suppose so," she admitted. "That is what Kay is always telling me. It would just about kill her father and me if anything happened to Kay. She is all we have left. My sister, who was Kay's mother, died when Kay was a little girl; and I have always had the care of her; so that she is just as dear to me as though she were my own."

"I can see how that is," said Marvel. "You sure ought to be mighty proud of yourself, Miss Pruell," he added.

"Why?" she asked. "What do you mean?"

"Kay is such a fine girl," he explained.

"She is a fine girl," said Miss Pruell, "whether I had anything to do with making her one or not; but the trouble with Kay is she is too trusting. She thinks everybody is just as fine as she is. She is self reliant enough; but somehow she doesn't seem to be as sophisticated as some of the other girls, and I am always afraid that she is going to be imposed upon."

"Now no one would have to worry if Dora Crowell was riding without a chaperon," suggested Marvel, "and she's a mighty nice girl, too."

"Dora impresses one as being able to take care of herself," said Miss Pruell.

"Well, Kay can take care of herself, too," said Marvel. "Oh shucks, Miss Pruell, she'll be all right."

"Oh, I know it," admitted the woman, "but just the same I'd feel safer if you'd been along, Mr. Marvel."

He looked at her in surprise. "But I'm more of a stranger than Cory," he reminded her.

"I know what Kay thinks of you," she said. "We have both felt that she was so much safer when you were along since what you did that day."

"I'm very glad to know that you have confidence in me," said the man.

"Yes, we both have a lot of confidence in you, Mr. Marvel, especially Kay. She was all broken up this morning when she told me you were going away."

He made no reply; but he was thinking that the girl had very successfully hidden her regret from him; but then girls were funny. He had read enough about them in books to know that. Everyone said they were funny.

"I guess I won't ever understand them," he said.

"Who?" she asked.

"Did I say anything? I must have been thinking out loud." He was looking out across the ranch yard down the valley; but his thoughts were in the other direction, where a golden haired girl in overalls rode with a man he did not trust. "Here comes a car," he said. "You don't see many cars up here."

Miss Pruell looked up. "Why bless my heart," she exclaimed, "I believe that's Mr. White. Yes, that's Kay's father. I recognize his roadster."

The two sat watching the approaching car as it came swiftly up the rough road and, slowing down, turned into the ranch yard. Then Miss Pruell stood up and waved her hand, and as the car stopped before the house she went down the steps to greet a well built man of fifty with graying hair that accentuated the bronze of his tanned face.

"Hello Abbie," he said.

"I am so glad you've come, John."

"Where is Kay?" he demanded.

"She's out for the day — gone on a paper chase." He had opened up the rumble seat and was getting out his bags.

"Can't I help you, sir?" asked Marvel, coming down the steps.

"John, this is Mr. Marvel," said Miss Pruell. "This is Kay's father, Mr. Marvel."

The two men shook hands; and in the brief keen scrutiny of the instant, each saw something in the other that he liked.

"Mr. Marvel saved Kay's life the other day, John."

"They are going to make a good story of that before they get through with it," said Marvel laughing; but he had to listen again to a detailed narration of the whole affair.

"I'm sorry that I can't tell you how I feel about this," said John White; "but until you are a father yourself you can't understand what I owe you."

After helping White in with his bags, Marvel left the two and strolled down to the stable, guessing that they might probably have much of a personal nature to discuss; so that he did not see them again until dinner was served at noon.

During the conversation at the table, Marvel learned that John White had started in life as a cowpuncher, that he had become foreman of a big ranch in California and then a partner; and that with the accumulation of wealth and the growth of the community in which he lived, he had drifted into banking. It seemed almost like a fairy story to Marvel, and he wanted to ask a great many questions; but his natural reticence prevented, and presently the conversation drifted to other topics; and soon the meal was over and Butts was calling him from the veranda.

"You better shake a leg, Mister, if you're goin' along with me," he said.

"Just a moment, my man," replied Marvel; but he rose from the table. "I'll say goodbye before I leave," he said to Miss Pruell and White. "It will take a few minutes to get my baggage roped on to the buckboard."

When he reached the veranda, Butts met him with a surly scowl. "Give me a hand with my stuff, Butts," he said.

"Hustle it yourself," growled the cowpuncher. "I aint flunkyin' for no tenderfoot."

"Have it your own way," said Marvel. "I aint in any hurry to leave; but I don't leave without my trunk, and I aint goin' to carry it alone. If Blaine finds me here when he gets back he's goin' to be peeved at you."

Butts hesitated for a moment, and then he growled something under his breath.

"Come on then," he said. "Where is it? I don't want to see you around here no longer than I have to."

Together they went to Bruce's room and carried his trunk and bag out to the buckboard; and while Butts was roping the baggage on to the vehicle, Marvel returned to the house and bid Miss Pruell and Mr. White goodbye.

"I hope I see you again some time, young man," said White, as they parted.

"You don't hope it half as much as I do," thought Marvel as he turned and left them.

"Well, are you about ready?" demanded Butts.

"Just as soon as I get Baldy," said Marvel.

"What you goin' to do with Baldy?" demanded the cowpuncher.

"I'm goin' to lead him down to the railroad."

"Who said so?"

"I do."

"You aint goin' to lead him behind this buck-board," said Butts.

"Then I stay right here. Take my trunk off."

"Well you got me again," said Butts, "but you're sure goin' to be sorry for it."

"Not if I know it," replied Marvel.

"Goodbye, Mr. Marvel," called Miss Pruell, who had come out onto the veranda. "I hope you have a pleasant trip."

"I'm expecting to," replied Bruce.

Butts drove down to the stable; and Marvel went in and led Baldy out, taking him up close to the side of the off horse.

"What you doin' there?" demanded Butts.

"I'm goin' to tie him up here where you can't get funny and lose him," replied Marvel.

"You know too damned much for a tenderfoot," said Butts.

"He'll travel better up here anyway," said Marvel, "besides removin' all temptation from your soul."

After he had tied Baldy's halter rope to the ring in the snaffle bit of the off horse, he came back and climbed into the buckboard and Butts started the team toward town.

At first Baldy was inclined to make things awkward; and Butts indulged in much grumbling and profanity, but after awhile the horse settled down to the gait of his fellows and thereafter travelled easily.

From the ranch stable to the little town sprawling along the railroad, two and a half hours away, neither man spoke, except that at the end of the journey Marvel told Butts to leave him and his stuff off at the hotel; for the next eastbound train did not leave until early in the morning.

The westbound train on which Butts expected his passengers was late — how late the station agent could not tell.   All he knew was that it was held up by a wrecked freight train, and that it might be several hours before the track was cleared.

Marvel got a room in the hotel and took Baldy to the livery stable.

The proprietor of the livery was a bleary eyed, red nosed individual, who appeared much interested in Marvel's clothes.

"I reckon you be one of Cory Blaine's dudes," he said.

"Do you?" inquired Marvel politely.

"Your horse?" asked the proprietor.

"Yes.   You haven't got a saddle and bridle you want to sell, have you?"

"I've got an outfit I've been holdin' for a board bill for more'n a year now," replied the proprietor.   He took the halter rope from Marvel and led Baldy into a stall.

"What you feedin'?" asked Marvel.

"I got some good alfalfa hay."

"Nothing else?" asked Bruce.

"What you want for this cayuse?   T-bone steaks?"

"I seen some oat hay stacked in the shed when I come in," said Marvel.   "Give him that."

"You're sure particular."

"Just like you would be with one of your horses," said Bruce. "I know a horseman when I see him, and I'll bet yours get nothing but the best."

The bleary eyed one swelled perceptibly. "You're dead right, young feller," he said.

"And where's your grain?" demanded Marvel.

"Grain?"

"Sure. You can't never make me think a man like you don't grain his horses. Oh, I see. It's in that bin back there. You fork him in some of that oat hay, and I'll get the grain;" and he started toward the end of the barn where the grain bin stood.

The proprietor hesitated; then he shook his head and went outside to fork the hay into Baldy's manger. When he returned Bruce had already measured out a generous ration of oats for his horse.

"Now let me see that outfit," he said.

Ten minutes later he had purchased an old but serviceable saddle, to the pommel of which was tied a forty foot hemp rope, had also acquired a bridle of sorts, and was on his way back to his hotel room.

xiv

Kidnaped

As Cory Blaine, with Kay and Bud, rode
away from the ranch house ahead of the others,
they bore to the southwest through a low pass that
took them out of the main valley in which the
ranch lay.

At the horn of his saddle, Bud carried a sack
filled with paper cut into small pieces; and some
of this he dropped occasionally as Blaine instructed him to do so.

"You might as well ride on ahead, Bud," said

Cory. "Follow that old, dry spring trail for about five miles and then cut across to the left, back into the valley. Drop a little paper when you enter a main trail; and then you don't have to drop no more, as long as the trail is plain, until you leave it. After you leave a trail, ride about fifty yards before you drop any more paper. That'll make 'em hunt around a bit to pick up your trail again. After you get into the valley, keep out of sight as much as possible. Use washes and high brush to hide yourself, and keep on up the valley quite a bit before you cross. I don't care if you go as far as Mill Creek. We're goin' to give 'em a ride today that they'll remember."

"If I go that roundabout way to Mill Creek," said Bud, "it'll be nigh on to forty miles before we get back to the ranch."

"I don't believe some of us can stand it," said Kay.

"They'll have somethin' to talk about for the rest of their lives," said Cory, "and that's what most of 'em are out here for. It won't kill 'em."

"Bert Adams won't never sit down again," said Bud.

"That's his funeral," said Blaine. "You mosey

along now, Bud; and we'll follow. You got the best horse in the outfit, and there aint no use of our tryin' to keep up with you."

"All right," said Bud. "So long," and he rode away.

Blaine held his horse to a walk until Bud was out of sight. He did not talk to the girl, who followed behind him along the narrow trail, but presently she spoke to him.

"You're off the trail, Cory," she said. "This isn't the main trail, and Bud hasn't dropped any paper."

"Oh, that's all right," said Cory. "I know where Bud's ridin' and this is an easier way. It's a short cut."

"I don't see how it can be a short cut," said the girl, "when it's bearing off to the west, while Mill Creek is southeast of us."

"Well, it aint shorter in distance, Kay," he said; "but it's a whole lot easier, and we'll make better time. The trail Bud's on gets mighty rough a bit farther up, and we'll dodge all that and may even beat him into the valley."

They dropped down into a gully and crossed a low ridge, beyond which lay a barren and forbidding gulch, carved from the red soil by the rains of ages.

It did not look like an easier way to Kay; but she had confidence in Blaine's knowledge of the country and was content to follow where he led.

A steep and precarious cattle trail led down into the bottom of the gulch, where they were entirely hidden from view in the winding bed of a dry wash.

"What a lonely place," said Kay.

Blaine made no reply.   He was unusually quiet and preoccupied.

Despite herself, the girl felt nervous.   She wished now that she had insisted upon continuing on with Bud; and then she noticed for the first time that Cory carried no gun, as was habitually his custom.

"You forgot your gun," she said.

"That's right," he replied, "I did.   I was so busy this morning I must o' plumb forgot it."

"I don't like this place, Cory," she said after another silence.   "I wish you'd take me out of it."

They were crossing the mouth of another deep wash that entered that in which they were riding. The sides of these washes were unusually perpendicular and sometimes ten or fifteen feet in height, forming narrow, tortuous corridors, their walls broken occasionally by well worn cattle trails that led down one bank and up the other.

Something attracted Kay's attention up the wash they were passing. "Cory!" she exclaimed in a startled whisper. "I saw a man up there. He had a handkerchief tied across his face."

Just ahead of them the wash turned abruptly to the left, and the girl had scarcely ceased speaking when a rider blocked their further progress. He, too, wore a bandana about the lower part of his face, hiding all but his eyes.

"Stick 'em up," he said.

Cory's hands went up; and at the same instant Kay wheeled Lightfoot in an effort to escape; for in that instant she sensed that she had been led into a trap.

Quick though her action was, it was too late, for as Lightfoot wheeled, the other rider spurred into the wash, blocking her escape.

"Set tight, Miss," he said, covering her with his forty-five.

"Climb down!" ordered the man confronting Blaine.

"What do you want?" asked Cory. "If it's money, take what you want. I aint armed."

"Shut up and climb down," growled the bandit.

Cory did as he was bid, and the man also dismounted and came toward him. "Turn around," he said, "and don't make no funny moves if you don't want to get kilt."

He took the riata from Blaine's saddle, had the man lower his arms behind his back and then secured his wrists there with one end of the rope. Looping the reins of Blaine's horse over the horn of his own saddle, he turned back up the wash leading his horse, while Blaine followed at the end of the rope, with Kay and her captor trailing in the rear.

Around the bend a cattle trail led up onto the bank, and here the party climbed out of the wash and halted beside a clump of high bushes. Here the man who had Cory in charge made the latter lie down and quickly bound his ankles, after which he removed Blaine's bandana from about his throat, twirled it into a cylinder, the center of which he made Blaine take in his mouth, after which he tied the ends tightly at the back of his neck, effectually gagging him.   Then he tied the prostrate man's horse to the other side of the bush.

"I reckon they'll find you in a couple of days," he said.

In the meantime the other man had taken down Kay's halter rope and was holding it to prevent another attempt at escape.

"What are you going to do with me?"

"You're goin' along with us, Miss," said the man who had been tying up Cory.   "As long as you don't get to actin' up, you won't get hurt." Then he mounted, and the three rode up the gulch toward the south.

It was five o'clock in the afternoon when Bud rode into the ranch yard, unsaddled his pony, and turned it out to pasture.   As he walked toward the bunk house, Miss Pruell called to him from the veranda, where she was sitting with John White.

"Where are the rest of them?" she asked, when he had come over.

"I guess they aint far behind," he said.   "I seen 'em a couple of times."

"I thought Kay and Cory were with you," said Miss Pruell.

"They dropped behind the first thing this morning," said Bud, "and I haven't seen 'em since. I reckon they'll be in directly though."

A half hour later the other riders commenced to straggle in. Dora Crowell was first; and fifteen minutes later the Talbots appeared and joined them on the veranda.

Miss Pruell had introduced John White first to Dora and then to the Talbots; and of each he had inquired about Kay, but none of them had seen either her or Cory.

"Look there," exclaimed White, pointing up the valley. "Here comes a riderless horse."

"That is probably Adams'," said Benson Talbot. "The last time I saw him he looked like he'd a whole lot rather walk than ride."

Bud was standing at the foot of the steps and now he strained his eyes through the growing dusk. "That aint Adams' horse," he said. "That's Cory's. Somethin' must have happened."

With the exception of Miss Pruell and Birdie Talbot, they all went down to the corral to meet the horse as he came trotting in. The animal was dragging his halter rope, the loose end of which was knotted about a bit of broken brush wood.

"Cory had him tied and he busted loose," said Bud. "I reckon he's walkin' in and that Miss White is stayin' with him."

"Why didn't they continue on with you?" demanded White.

"That's just what I'd like to know," said Bud. "I can't figure it out."

"Did the rest of you follow this man's trail all the way?" asked White, turning to Talbot.

"Yes," replied Talbot, "it was plainly marked; and I think we never got off of it once."

"Then if they weren't considerably off the trail you should have seen something of them," continued White. "There is something wrong here. It doesn't look good to me at all."

"It doesn't look good to me either, Mr. White," said Dora Crowell, "and there is something wrong."

"We should send out after them at once," continued White. "How many men have you here?" he turned to Bud.

"There's me and two other fellers," said Bud. "We'll start right out if you say so."

"I wish you would," replied White; "and you will be well rewarded if you find them."

"We'll have to catch up some fresh horses," said Bud. "We'll find them all right, Mr. White. Don't worry." He turned to the two men in the corral. "Get up the horses," he said, "and get saddled up. I want to get a snack of grub before I start. I aint had nothin' to eat all day."

When he had departed in the direction of the kitchen, Dora Crowell drew John White to one side. "I don't want to alarm you unnecessarily, Mr. White," she said; "but if I were you I wouldn't trust entirely to these men. There's a deputy sheriff down in town. I think you should telephone him to start a posse out after them."

"Do you think that it is as serious as that?" he asked.

"I don't know," she said; "but if you were not here, I should have done it myself."

"You must have some grounds for your suspicions," he said. "I wish that you would be frank with me."

"Blaine is in love with your daughter," said Dora; "and," she added, "I don't think that he is any too trustworthy."

"Does she care for him?" he asked.

"No, and that is where the danger lies."

"Where is the telephone?" asked White.

"In the office," replied Dora. "Come with me, and I'll show you where it is."

As the two returned to the ranch house, Bert Adams rode into the yard and up to the corral. He was swaying in the saddle when his horse came to a stop. Painfully and laboriously, he dismounted; then he lay down in the dirt, while his horse walked on into the stable.

Bruce Marvel was sitting in the office of the hotel in the little cow town when the telephone bell rang. The proprietor was washing his face in a tin basin just outside the door. His hands and his hair and his eyes and his nose and his mouth were covered with lather. "Will you answer the danged thing for me, young feller?" he asked; and in compliance with the request Bruce crossed to the instrument.

"Hello!" he said, as he took down the receiver.

"Hello!" said a voice at the other end. "This is John White at the TF Ranch. I want to speak to the deputy sheriff."

"Wait a minute," said Bruce, and then turning to the proprietor "Here's a fellow wants to talk with the deputy sheriff," he said.

"He's out to his ranch, and he aint got no telephone. Take the message."

"I can't get hold of him now," said Marvel into
the transmitter, "but if you'll give me your message I'll get it to him."

"My daughter and Cory Blaine are lost somewhere in the hills," said White. "They went out
on a paper chase early this morning. Every one
else is in but them. Blaine's horse came in alone
five minutes ago. I want the sheriff to form a
posse and make a thorough search for them. I'll
stand all the expenses and pay a reward in addition."

Marvel was almost stunned by the informa-
tion, but his voice showed no indication of excitement as he answered. "One man will start right
now, Mr. White," he said, "and the sheriff will
be notified to follow with a posse. Good bye,"
and he hung up without waiting to hear more.

In a few brief words he explained the situation
to the hotel proprietor. "Can you get word to
the sheriff at once?" he asked.

"I'll have a man on the road in five minutes."

"Good. And now listen to me. Tell 'em never
to mind huntin' the hills. Ride straight to Hi

Bryam's shack at the head of Mill Creek canyon. If they don't find nuthin' there, tell 'em to keep on along the One Mile Creek trail to Kelly's place in Sonora."

"You seem to know a lot about this here country for a tenderfoot," commented the proprietor.

"Never mind what I know. Get busy," and, turning, he took the steps two at a time to his room on the second floor.

Quickly he stripped off his clothes, and opening his trunk dragged out well worn boots and spurs, overalls, flannel shirt, Stetson, chaps and bandana. Quickly he donned them, and then strapped about his hips a cartridge belt that supported two old forty-fours in holsters as darkened and mellowed by age as were his chaps and his cartridge belt.

As he ran down the stairs, crossed the office and stepped out into the night, no one saw him, for the proprietor had gone to find a man to send after the sheriff. The train from the east was pulling into the station; and Butts was waiting for his passengers; so that he did not see Marvel as the latter hurried to the stable as Olga Gunderstrom alighted from the train.

No one was at the livery stable as Marvel entered and saddled and bridled Baldy, for the proprietor was eating his supper in his home across the street.

Earlier in the afternoon, while it was still light, Marvel had noticed a pile of empty gunny sacks on the floor beside the grain bin. Into one of these he dumped several measures of oats, tied the sack securely back of his saddle and a moment later rode out into the night toward the south.

XV

ONE HUNDRED THOUSAND DOLLARS

BUTTS' NONE too lovely disposition had been badly strained by his enforced wait for the delayed train. There were urgent reasons why he should have been back at the ranch early; and now as he wrestled with two trunks and three suit cases in an endeavor to strap them all securely to the back of the buckboard, he inwardly cursed everything and everybody that came out of the East, and especially the supercilious young woman who spoke to him in the same tone of

voice as she had addressed the colored porter as
she tipped him at the Pullman steps. But at last
he had everything tied on securely; and then he
turned to the girl, "Get in, Miss," he said
brusquely; and when she had seated herself beside him "You better hang on tight. We're goin'
to travel."

Once across the railroad tracks he gave the
bronchos a cut with the whip; and as they
bounded forward, Olga Gunderstrom's head
snapped back.

"Mercy!" she exclaimed. "Please be more
careful, my man."

Butts gritted his teeth and struck the horses
again.

"I shall report you for this," snapped the young
lady.

"Report and be blowed," snapped Butts. "I'm
sick of this job anyway. I'm fed up on dudes and
dudesses."

A short distance out of town they passed a lone
horseman who spurred his horse to one side of
the road as they dashed past. Out of the corner
of his eye Butts saw the rider; but so quickly did
he pass that he recognized nothing familiar in

the figure, which is not surprising, though had he been able to note the horse more closely he would doubtless have found much that was familiar about him.

It was a dusty and angry young woman who alighted from the buckboard at the foot of the TF Ranch house steps. Dora Crowell recognized her immediately and ran down to greet her.

"Why, Olga Gunderstrom!" she cried. "Cory Blaine never told me you were coming today."

"Well, here I am," snapped Olga; "and it's no fault of this man here that I am here alive. I never saw such a surly, impudent person in my life. Where is Mr. Blaine? He ought to discharge him at once."

"Mr. Blaine is missing," said Dora. "We are afraid that something has happened to him and Miss White in the hills. Did you hear what I said, Butts?"

"Yes, I heard you, Miss," replied the man, who received the news without any show of excitement.

"Bud and the other two boys have gone out to search for them," continued Dora. "Don't you think you better go too, Butts?"

"That's what I'm aimin' on doin'," replied the man. "If there was anything here but dudes I could get started right away, but I've got to unload all this junk and then put the team away."

"We'll attend to that," said John White. "I'll certainly be glad to have another man who knows the hills out looking for them."

As he came down the steps toward the buckboard, Benson Talbot arose. "I'll help you, Mr. White," he said.

"I'd like to," murmured Bert Adams weakly, "but I don't think I can get up."

"We can manage it all right, I guess," said White.

"Thanks!" mumbled Butts ungraciously, as he started for the corral.

The only horses up were the sorrel colt and the old horse that was used to drive in the saddle horses; and Butts, being for some reason, in a great hurry, saddled the former. He rode straight toward the west, crossed two ridges and dropped down into a dry wash.

After he reached the bottom of the wash, he commenced to whistle occasionally, a few bars from an old time air that had once been popular.

Presently, from the distance, it came down to him again like an echo. He urged the sorrel into a faster walk, and a few minutes later a voice hailed him.

"Hey, you!" it called. "I'm up here on the bank."

Butts found the trail that led up from the bottom of the wash, and a moment later he dismounted beside Cory Blaine.

"You long eared idiot!" exclaimed Blaine. "Did you figure I expected to be left here all the rest of my life? The next time I pick a man for a job like this, it won't be you."

"I couldn't help it," said Butts. "The train was late, held up by a wreck. I run the broncs all the way from the railroad and then started right out after you. I aint had nuthin' to eat, either."

"That's too bad about you," grumbled Blaine, as Butts fumbled with the knot of the rope that secured his ankles and wrists. "I've been lying here all day with nothing to eat and nothing to drink."

"What happened to your horse? They say he came in just before dark?"

"The damn fool got frightened at somethin' and pulled back 'till he busted the brush he was tied to; then he beat it."

"Everything work all right?" asked Butts.

"Sure, all except this. I sure didn't aim on lyin' here all day and half the night."

"You should have brung a bed," said Butts.

"Do you think that sorrel will carry double?" asked Blaine.

"I reckon he's gonna have to," said Butts, "for I sure aint goin' to walk."

"Maybe we'll both have to walk," said Blaine.

"We'll try it down in the bottom of the wash," said Butts. "If he started pitchin' up on the bank here he'd be sure to fall in."

"Let me have him," said Blaine. "You can ride behind."

"I always get the worst of it," said the other.

Cory mounted and rode down into the wash, reining the sorrel close to a low spot along the bank, from which Butts lowered himself gingerly onto the animal's rump.

"I guess he aint goin' to do nuthin'," said Blaine.

"I hope not," said Butts.

"I suppose there is a lot of excitement at the ranch," said Blaine, as the sorrel walked off like an old family horse.

"I guess they is," said Butts. "I wasn't there long. Her father came today."

Blaine whistled. "Has he offered a reward?" he asked.

"He'll give a reward all right, but he didn't say how much."

"Well, it's goin' to be plenty," said Blaine, "unless —— "

"Unless what?" asked Butts.

"When I pull this rescue stunt from Kelly's ranch, I won't want no reward or ransom money nor nuthin', if she'll marry me; for if I'm ever John White's son-in-law, I'll be sittin' pretty for the rest of my life."

"But how about the rest of us?" asked Butts. "Where do we come in? We aint goin' to be no son-in-laws, and we want our cut of the ransom."

"That's so," said Blaine, scratching his head. "Well, I reckon he'll have to pay the ransom; but he won't have to pay no reward."

"You be a regular hero and refuse to take it," said Butts. "That'll make a hit with him."

"But I still get my cut of the ransom," Blaine reminded him.

"I don't care what you get as long as I get mine," and then they rode on in silence for some time.

"I'd hate to trust my girl to that bunch," said Butts, "especially Hi Bryam."

"They know I'd kill 'em," said Blaine.

"Well, she's your girl," said Butts; "but I wouldn't trust Bryam, at least not way down in Mexico where he could make his getaway."

"I aint worryin' none," said Blaine, and then as though the subject bored him, "Did that Marvel fellow get away today?" he asked.

"Say, don't mention that son-of-a-gun's name to me. Every time I think of him I could chaw the head off a rattlesnake."

"There was somethin' fishy about him," said Blaine. "He sure had me worried. Did I ever tell you how he rid this colt?"

"I knew he took him when he went to look for them fool horse's teeth," said Butts.

"I was watchin' him when he rid away, and I seen this little son-of-a-gun start to pitch down there just before the road makes the big bend around the hill. He sure gave that dude the works, but it never seemed to faze him; and when he come in that night, sayin' he's been lost, he swore the colt never did a thing and was gentle as a kitten."

"I can't figure it out," said Butts. "Maybe it was just an accident, and then again maybe he kin ride, but he sure can't shoot; and he aint got real good sense, either — huntin' for horse's teeth."

"Did he ever find a tooth?" asked Blaine.

"He found a whole mouth full of 'em in that pinto o' yourn; but it stunk so that Bud said he lost interest, real sudden like, and wouldn't even look for no more."

"He sure was a damn fool," said Blaine, "throwin' my boot away. I think he done it apurpose."

"And shootin' a hole in his bedroll," scoffed Butts. "That dude sure was loco."

"I wish I was sure he was a dude," said Blaine.

"What do you think he was?" demanded Butts.

"I dunno," said Blaine; "but he sure was the funniest dude I ever seen, if he was a dude."

"Well, he's gone now. You won't never see him again."

"I hope not."

When Blaine and Butts rode into the yard at the home ranch they found a depressed and worried company gathered on the veranda of the big house.

Dora Crowell was the first to recognize him as the two rode up. "There's Cory now!" she exclaimed, and immediately the entire party came down the steps and surrounded him as he and Butts dismounted from the sorrel colt.

"What happened?" demanded John White. "Where is my daughter?"

"You are Mr. White?" asked Blaine; and without waiting for a reply, "Something terrible has happened, Mr. White," he said. "Two fellows stuck us up this morning. I was unarmed, and we didn't have a chance. I thought they just wanted money; so I didn't even try to make a fight, though it wouldn't have done no good if I had and maybe your daughter would have been shot during the rumpus. They bound and gagged me and then rode off with her. During the day I managed to work the gag out of my mouth, but I couldn't get my hands and feet loose."

"I found him tied up like a sack of barley over

in Dry Spring Gulch," said Butts. "If he hadn't of got that gag out, I'd of rid right by him in the dark."

"Which way did they take her?" asked White.

"They went west over the ridge," said Blaine.

"I wish we had known that sooner," said White, "the sheriff was just here with a posse; and it might have helped him to know which way they went."

"Which way was he aimin' to look?" asked Blaine.

"He wouldn't tell me," said White. "He just said that he had a tip. They only stopped here long enough to see if we'd heard anything, and then they rode on."

"How did the sheriff hear of it?" asked Blaine.

"I telephoned to town just as soon as it was obvious that something must have happened to you and Kay," explained White.

Cory seemed thoughtful. "I wonder where he got his tip and what it is?"

Butts had departed, taking the sorrel colt to the stable. "Ask one of the boys to get Blue up for me, Butts," Blaine called after him.

"None of the boys are here," said Dora.

"They are all out looking for you and Kay."

"I'll get him up," said Butts.

"What are you going to do?" asked White.

"I'm goin' out to look for your daughter, Mr. White," replied Cory, "and I'll never come back until I find her."

"It will mean ten thousand dollars, Mr. Blaine, to you or any other man that brings her back alive," said White.

"I don't want no money, sir," Blaine assured him. "It means more to me than all the money in the world to get her back to you safe and sound. I feel like it was all my fault that this happened."

"Don't take it too hard, Blaine," said White generously. "I don't see what you could have done to prevent it."

"I'm all broke up over it," said Blaine, "but by God, sir, I'll get her back; and if anything's happened to her, somebody's goin' to get kilt."

"Whoever they are," said White, "you may rest assured that they shall be brought to justice. I have already telegraphed to business associates in Mexico and to the sheriffs of adjoining counties to be on the lookout. If they get away, it will be a miracle."

For a moment Cory Blaine stood in thoughtful meditation.

"Perhaps that wasn't the right thing to do, Mr. White," he suggested. "Them sort of fellers is desperate. If they're surrounded they might make away with her in some lonely spot and bury her where she wouldn't never be found in a hundred years; then they could scatter, and even if some of 'em was caught, it would be hard to prove anything on 'em; for they was masked and I couldn't never identify 'em. If I was you I would telegraph all them people to lay off for awhile 'till I see what I can do. I know this country better than anyone, and if I can't find her nobody can."

"I'll think over what you have said," replied White noncommittally.

"I reckon I'll go and get me something to eat," said Cory. "I aint eat since breakfast, and I may not get a chance to eat again for some time."

As he ran up the steps and entered the house, some of the party returned to the veranda; but John White detained Dora Crowell. "Don't you think now that you were mistaken about Blaine?" he asked. "He certainly had no part in the abduction, and it is evident that he is terribly cut up about it."

"Nevertheless, Mr. White, if I were you, I wouldn't call off those telegrams," said Dora. "If those men are so desperate, they are not going to let Cory Blaine take Kay away from them single-handed."

"I guess you are right at that," said White, "and it won't hurt to give him all the help that we can get for him, but still I can't help having confidence in him."

"I wish I could," said Dora.

Butts had gotten the horses up, and after considerable difficulty he managed to get ropes on two of them. These he had saddled and tied to the corral posts, and then he had gone to the bunk house.

Rummaging in the duffle bag that was tucked beneath his cot, he finally extracted a piece of note paper. The bunkhouse was dark, and no one had seen him enter it from the veranda of the ranch house; nor did they see him emerge, but presently they saw him hurrying excitedly toward them.

"Look here," he cried as he reached the foot

of the steps. "Here's a note from the kidnapers. It was stuck to the side of the bunkhouse door."

White took the slip of paper from him eagerly and, followed by the others, went into the ranch house where, by the light of the kerosene lamp, he deciphered the crude scrawl.

"Tell Mr. White," it read, "that if he wants to see his daughter alive again to have one hundred thousand dollars in twenty dollar bills ready one week from today at TF Ranch. He will get further instructions then how to deliver the money and get his girl. No funny business or we'll slit her throat."

There was no signature, and the characters were printed in an obvious effort to disguise the hand.

Cory Blaine had eaten, and as he joined them White handed him the note. "What do you think of it?" asked White, after Blaine had read it.

"Where did it come from?" demanded Blaine.

"I found it stickin' on the side of the bunk house beside the door," said Butts. "It sure gave me a shock when I read it."

"How could you read it?" asked Dora Crowell. "There is no light at the bunkhouse."

Just for an instant Butts' jaw dropped. Perhaps no one noticed it, for he caught himself so quickly. "I seen the paper and I struck a match," he said.

"Oh!" was Dora's only comment.

"What would you advise, Blaine?" asked White.

"I might fail, Mr. White," replied Cory; "and after all the first thing we care about is getting Kay back, so maybe you better get the money in case I do fail."

"If you get in touch with them, Blaine, you may offer them the reward in my name," said White. "It is a great deal of money; but I think that I can raise it; and, of course, it is needless to say that I would make any sacrifice to get Kay back alive and well."

"I'll sure do all I can, Mr. White," said Cory. "You may absolutely depend on me."

"I got two horses up, Cory," said Butts. "I'm goin' with you."

"You stay here," said Blaine. "I don't need no help, and if any other clew should turn up while I'm gone there ought to be someone here who knows the country and who can ride hard."

Butts said nothing, but he accompanied Blaine as he walked down to the stable for his horse. "One of us has got to be here," said Cory. "If anything goes wrong and it aint safe for me to return, light a fire on the hill. I'll make a signal on Horsecamp Butte on my way back. You keep your eye peeled for it, and if I don't get no signal from you that night I'll know that everything is jake and I'll come on in."

"All right," said Butts, "but I hate to have to hang around here. I feel sort of nervous."

"Why?"

"That Crowell girl. She came near getting me. I sure do hate all them damn dudes."

"Keep your mouth shut, and you won't get in trouble," advised Blaine.

A minute later he had mounted and ridden off into the night.

XVI

AT BRYAM'S CABIN

BRUCE MARVEL conserved the energies of his
horse, for he knew that he might have a gruelling
grind ahead of him. His, he realized, was an en-
durance race in which speed might readily prove
a liability rather than an asset; for were he to
reach his goal with an exhausted mount, failure
must be his only reward.

He believed that he was pitted against a hard
and desperate gang and that even should he be so
successful as to wrest Kay White from them, his

ability to return her in safety to the TF Ranch might still depend solely upon what of stamina and speed were left in Baldy.

He rode steadily until shortly after midnight when he dismounted and removing the horse's saddle and bridle permitted him to roll.

A short time previously he had watered him in Mill Creek; and now when he had stretched his muscles in a good roll and both of them had rested for five or ten minutes, Bruce gave the animal a small feed of oats; and after he had cleaned them up they were soon on the trail again.

All night he rode; and just before dawn he halted again for a brief rest, during which he re-moved the saddle and bridle from Baldy, rubbed down his back, turned the blanket and re-saddled immediately.

As he mounted he glanced back down the valley, his eyes immediately attracted by a twinkling light ten or a dozen miles away.

"That must be the sheriff and his posse," he thought, "for there wasn't nobody there when I came past."

And far up, toward the head of Mill Creek

Canyon, other eyes saw the light — the eyes of a watcher posted on the hillside above Hi Bryam's cabin. "Not so good," muttered the watcher, and, descending, he awakened two men who were sleeping outside the shack.

"What's wrong, Mart?" demanded one of them.

"They's a campfire this side of Mill Creek camp," replied the man. "I think we better be movin'. There shouldn't be nobody comin' this way that would build a campfire."

"Cory told us to rest here for one day."

"I don't care what he told us. I'm lookin' after my own neck, and I aint goin' to wait around here for no man."

"Me neither," said Bryam. "He sure give us credit for sense enough to get out of here if you fellows were followed, and it looks like you was, all right."

"It's all the same to me," said the third. "I aint hankerin' to have no one see me with this girl here, whether they're followin' us or not."

"He was just figurin' on givin' the girl a rest, thinkin' she couldn't stand so much ridin'," said the first speaker.

"She's had five hours rest now," said Bryam, "and that's all she's goin' to get for awhile. You and Mart get saddled up, while I rustle some grub. We got plenty time to eat and get a good start, even if they start now, which like as not they won't."

"Probably they'll be waitin' till mornin'," said Eddie, "thinkin' they could pick up our trail better then."

"That's sure a long way off," said Mart. "I don't see how you seen it in the first place, Eddie;" and, in truth, the distant campfire was little more than a glowing speck in the far distance. Only the keenest eyes could have detected it at all and even to such it did not burn steadily, but twinkled like a distant star of lesser magnitude.

"Well, you fellers get busy," said Bryam. "I'll wake the girl and get the grub."

"Better let her sleep as long as we can," said Eddie.

"The hell with her," said Bryam. "She aint no better than we are."

"She's a girl," said Eddie, "and we ought to treat her as decent as we can."

"Don't be so soft," snapped Bryam.

"I aint soft," said Eddie, "but I aint stuck on this business. Kidnapin' women aint never been my particular line of business."

"Quit beefin'," said Mart, "and come on;" and Eddie followed off into the darkness in search of the hobbled horses.

Bryam went to the cabin door and opened it. "Say, you!" he called. "Wake up. We're leavin'."

Wake up! Kay White had been sitting wide eyed through the long hours since they had brought her to Bryam's shack. She could scarcely have forced herself to lie down upon the filthy thing that Bryam called a bed, but she knew that even had she done so, she could not have slept. She felt physical fatigue; but her mind was too awake, too active to entertain any thoughts of sleep.

"Dya hear me?" demanded Bryam.

"I heard you," replied the girl. "I am ready."

"I'm fixin' some grub," said Bryam. "When it's ready, I'll call you."

The girl, sitting in the rickety chair before the rough table, made no reply, as her thoughts, bridging the interruption, attacked once more the tangled skein they sought to unravel. She had been able only to guess at the motive for her abduction, since her captors would tell her nothing; but the logical surmise was that she would be held for ransom.

In the first instant of her capture she had sensed intuitively that Cory Blaine had deliberately led her into the trap; but when she had seen how roughly they had treated him and how heartlessly they had left him bound and gagged in the desolate gulch, that theory had been somewhat shaken. Then, again and again, the idea had forced itself upon her that perhaps in some way Bruce Marvel was responsible. There had been something mysterious about him. Both she and Dora Crowell had sensed that. He certainly was not what he had tried to lead them to believe he was, and this fact furnished a substantial groundwork for her suspicion.

Yet always she put the thought aside, refusing to accept it; and when the two men had brought her to Hi Bryam's cabin, her suspicion settled once more upon Cory Blaine; yet why had Marvel chosen to leave the ranch at this particular time? That question troubled her, for she knew that he had been planning to remain longer. Could it be that the paper chase had given him the opportunity for which he had been waiting. She remembered his refusal to accompany the party to Crater Mountain and that this refusal had followed the announcement that the paper chase would take place the following day and what a silly excuse he had given for remaining at the ranch—hunting horse's teeth indeed! Added to all this was the fact that he had quickly given up his search for teeth and had absented himself alone from the ranch for hours; but further than that she could never pursue this line of thought, since it invariably stopped before the blank wall of unreasoning belief in the integrity of the man.

"He could not have done it," she murmured. She sprang to her feet almost defiantly and raised her eyes to the black shadows among the rafters. "He did not do it," she said aloud.

"What's that?" asked Bryam from beyond the doorway.

She walked out to where the man stood beside the fire. "Cory Blaine did this," she said, "and you may tell him for me that there are two men in the world, one of whom will kill him for it — the one who catches him first."

"Blaine had nothing to do with it," snapped Bryam. "Here's the grub and you better eat. You got a long ride ahead of you."

In silence she ate the rough fare, for she knew that she must maintain her strength; and the three men with her ate, too, in silence, while the hounds nosed among them, whining for scraps.

"What you goin' to do with the pooches, Hi?" asked Mart, after he had finished eating.

"Leave 'em here," replied Bryam. "They can rustle plenty grub in the hills."

"Won't they follow us?" asked Eddie.

"Not if I tell 'em to stay here," replied Bryam.

"I've been thinkin'," said Mart suddenly.

"That aint one of the things that nobody aint expectin' of you," said Bryam.

"You listen," said the other.

"I'm listenin'."

"That campfire down there has upset all our plans. Everybody knows you're batchin' up here, huntin' lion. If they find you gone and your dogs here, that'll look funny to 'em."

"Well, what's to be done about it?"

"You ought to stay here," continued Mart. "It will be a whole lot safer for you and for us, too."

"How do you make that out?" demanded Bryam.

"If they find you here they aint goin' to suspicion you, are they?"

"No. That's right, too."

"And if you're here when they come, you can send them off on a wrong trail after us."

"That's where your head aint no good," said Bryam. "If you come here with the girl, then I must have known somethin' about it; and if you didn't come here, how could I tell 'em what trail you went on?"

"You don't have to tell 'em the girl was here. Tell 'em two fellers you never seen before rid in over the ridge from the east, bummed some grub and asked the trail to Deming; then say that they rid back up over the ridge to the east."

"That would be a hell of a trail to Deming," said Bryam.

"Sure it would," agreed Mart; "but don't you see that fellers stealin' the girl would just naturally beat it for the roughest country they could find?"

"That aint such a bad scheme," said Eddie.

"It's a durn good one," admitted Bryam.

"We'll ride up the canyon a bit, then cut across to the west ridge and follow that to the One Mile Creek Trail. You can easy brush out our trail above camp for a ways, then ride your horse up the east trail to the summit, come down somewhere else and ride him up again, pickin' another new place to come down into camp. That'll give a fresh horse trail to the east summit, and they aint goin' to stop to try and figure out whether there were two horses or three went up, even if they could tell, which probably they couldn't."

"You aint such a fool as you look," admitted Bryam grudgingly.

"Well, let's get started," said Eddie. "Come on, Miss, here's your horse."

"May I go back into the cabin a moment?" asked Kay. "I left my handkerchief there I think."

"Well hurry up," said Bryam.

She ran quickly into the cabin, but she did not search for any handkerchief. Instead she gath-

ered up a deck of greasy playing cards that had
been lying on the table and slipped them into the
pocket of her leather coat. A moment later she
was outside again and had mounted.

Mart led the way up the canyon, his horse following the trail in the darkness. Directly behind
him rode Kay, and following her was Eddie.
They had temporarily, at least, discarded their
original plan of leading Kay's horse, for it was
obvious that this would have been most difficult
upon the steep, rough trail, zig-zagging up the
canyonside to the summit of the western ridge.
They had warned her against the danger of at-
tempting to escape, since a single misstep from
the trail might result in injury or death to her;
and she knew that they were right.

In the darkness Kay took one of the playing
cards from her pocket and tied her handkerchief
tightly about it. When she saw Mart turn abruptly from the trail toward the ridge at their
right, she dropped the handkerchief and the card
to the ground, knowing there was no likelihood
that he would perceive what she had done. Then
she took another card from her pocket and tore
it in two, dropping the halves at intervals; and

so she marked their way until they entered the main trail leading up the hillside.

Perhaps no one would come that way to see. Perhaps, if they did, they might not interpret the significance of the signs that she had left; but if someone did chance to see and guess the truth, she knew that she had plainly blazed for such the trail of her abductors onward from Bryam's shack.

The trail, bad enough in the daytime, seemed infinitely worse at night, yet they reached the summit of the ridge in safety and were moving southward on more level ground.

With dogged determination, Bruce Marvel followed the trail upward into Mill Creek Canyon. Baldy had responded nobly to the call upon him; but as the man had done all that he could to conserve his horse's strength, the animal had not, as yet, shown indications of fatigue.

"Baldy, I'm banking on you," said the man in low tones. "You saved her once and you're going to again. If we find her at Bryam's, it won't be long now; but if they've left and hit the trail for Kelly's in Sonora, you and I got some ride cut out for us; but I reckon we can catch 'em, Baldy.

I seen their horses yesterday, and they aint one-two with you.   No, sir, old man, beside you they is just plain scrubs."

Once again he lapsed into his usual state of silence, but his mind was active with plans and memories.

He recalled, as he often did, Kay's tone of disgust when she had reproached him for having thrown Blaine's boot into the fire.   She had never spoken of it again, but he knew that she had not forgotten it and that by that much he had lowered himself in her estimation.   He admired her for not reverting to it again — another might have reminded him of it.   Yes, she was a brick all right.

xvii

Torn Playing Cards

Behind him, several hours now, rode the posse, headed by the deputy sheriff of Porico County; and behind the posse came Cory Blaine. He would have been glad to have passed them so that he might reach Bryam's shack first; but there seemed little likelihood that he would be able to do so; for they were maintaining a good gait and riding steadily, while a detour from the trail that would permit him to pass them unseen would necessitate negotiating rough terrain which could not but retard his own speed.

He cursed the luck that had brought John White to the ranch one day too soon and thus upset all his well laid plans, for he believed that if White had not been there Butts would have been able to have delayed the formation of a searching party until the following day at least.

And then, at last, in his darkest hour, fortune smiled upon him, for the posse halted to rest the horses.

Blaine did not know this until, unexpectedly, he saw a tiny fire glowing ahead of him, perhaps a half mile away. He watched it grow as he drew nearer until at last its leaping flame revealed the figures of men gathered about it.

"That," he said, "is what I call luck."

He reined his horse to the left, out of the trail, with the intention of passing around the posse, coming into the main trail again ahead of them.

Low hills, cut with washes, came close to Mill Creek at this point; and it was necessary for Blaine's horse to pick his way carefully through the darkness. Perhaps a better horseman, or a more considerate man, would have dismounted and led the animal; but Blaine, like many of his kind, was only a rider and no horseman; nor was he instinctively considerate of anything other than his own interests. He was tired, and so it pleased him to ride; and his horse, willing and obedient, did its best, though twice it nearly fell.

The two had covered half the distance of the detour and were opposite the camp of the posse when suddenly the bank of a dry wash gave way, precipitating horse and rider to the bottom. Fortunately for Blaine, he fell clear of the animal.

Scrambling to his feet, Cory approached his mount. Seizing the reins, he urged it up and it tried to respond to his command, but only fell back upon its side with a groan; then he cursed it beneath his breath and kicked it, and once again the creature struggled to arise. It almost succeeded this time and before it sank to earth again, the pale starlight had revealed to the man the hopelessness of its condition — a leg was broken.

For a moment Blaine stood in dumb, futile rage beside the beast; then, to his credit, he did the one merciful thing that he could do. Drawing his revolver, he shot the animal through the brain — a shot that brought every member of the posse to alert attention.

Far away, along the trail, the shot sounded faintly in the ears of a solitary horseman. He reined in and sat motionless for a full minute, listening; then he rode on, puzzled but not diverted from his course.

"Now what the hell was that?" exclaimed the deputy sheriff, who, with the other members of his posse, stepped quickly away from the fire at the sound of the shot.

"Hey, some of you fellers!" came a voice out of the darkness. "Come up here and give me a lift."

"Who are you?" demanded the deputy.

"Cory Blaine," came the reply.

The entire posse moved in the direction of Blaine. "What's the matter?" demanded one of them, after they had located the man in the bottom of the dry wash.

"I had to shoot my horse," replied Blaine. "He busted a leg. I tried to get my saddle off him, but the cinch ring caught somewhere underneath him. I need someone to give me a hand."

"What you doin' up here anyway?" demanded the deputy sheriff.

"I was followin' you fellers, and I guess I got

off the trail," replied Blaine. "It was sure dumb."

They helped him with his saddle, and he walked back to camp with it and his bridle.

"Will one of you fellers let me have a horse?" asked Blaine. The question apparently aroused no enthusiasm. "I got to get on," he said. "You see I feel more or less responsible for that girl."

"I don't reckon none of the boys want to hoof it back to town," said the deputy sheriff.

"I'll pay him a good price for his horse, if he will," insisted Blaine, "and he can pick up a fresh one at the ranch."

"I reckon," said the deputy sheriff, after another long silence, "that you better ride along double with one of us. Come mornin' we'll like as not run on to some range horses."

"I'll allow that's about the best we can do," said another; and so it was that when the posse took up the march again, following a considerable rest, Cory Blaine rode behind one of the men, while another packed his saddle, and a third carried his bridle.

Shortly after dawn, true to the deputy's prophecy, they sighted a bunch of range horses. Three of the men rode out from the posse and drove them in and shortly thereafter one of them had been roped and saddled; and once again, to his relief, Blaine had a mount.

To leave them and ride ahead now was impossible, for they were pushing their horses to the utmost; and though the animal he rode was fresh and could have outdistanced the others, perhaps, the deputy sheriff would not permit him to ride ahead of the posse, though his reasons therefor, prompted perhaps more by egotism than necessity, were vague.

Though he chafed beneath the authority of the officer, Blaine might still console himself with the knowledge that the trail up Mill Creek Canyon was often in plain sight from Bryam's shack, thus giving him the hope, that amounted almost to assurance, that the party there would see the posse in ample time to permit them to make good their escape.

Far up toward the head of Mill Creek Canyon, Hi Bryam sat in the doorway of his shack smoking his pipe. Far below him he saw the canyon spread out into a valley, through which Mill Creek wound, its tortuous course marked by the green of the verdure along its banks, standing out in bold relief against the purple and brown of the surrounding landscape. Little specks moved here and there upon the face of the valley. Grazing cattle and horses they were, and to the man they were just a part of the landscape, attracting no particular attention. But presently another speck appeared; and though to an unpracticed eye it might have appeared no different from the others, it brought Bryam to immediate and alert attention.

"That would be Blaine," he soliloquized. "I sorta got an idear he bit off more'n he can chaw this time. Somehow I wish I hadn't had nuthin' to do with it. Folks is funny that way. You can steal somebody's money and nobody seems to get terribly excited about it, except the feller whose money it was. But steal a woman or a kid and by God it's everybody's business, and they all want to kill you."

He sat for a long time watching the approaching horseman; and then he arose and went inside the cabin and returned with his rifle, an old Springfield thirty-thirty.

He sat down again with the weapon lying loosely across his knees, his eyes steadily upon the man and the horse drawing constantly nearer.

After awhile he arose again. "That don't look like Cory," he muttered. "I reckon I'd better hide out 'till I see who it is." He walked slowly toward a clump of trees, growing part way up on the side of the canyon, perhaps two hundred feet from the shack. His four hounds, lazing about near him, rose to follow. "Go on back, you," he said, and, obediently, they did as they were bid.

Bruce Marvel rode openly up to Bryam's shack, for he knew that it was useless to attempt to approach unseen. If anyone were there, eyes, he knew, had been watching him for many minutes; and he knew, too, that the best way to disarm suspicion was to avoid suspicious action. To ride up boldly would disarm them. He thought that Kay White was there; but he did not expect to see her, nor did he expect to take her away single-handed from three men. He did not believe that she was in any immediate danger, even though he still thought that Cory Blaine was with her; for he believed that Blaine's prime object was to collect a ransom and that he would not harm her as long as there was any hope of that.

On the way up he had made his plans very carefully. He had decided that he would tell whoever was there that Kay was lost and that he was looking for her. Bryam, or whoever else was there, would tell him, of course, that they knew nothing about it, that they had not seen her. Then he would ride on; but instead of following directly on the trail to Sonora, he would ride up to the ridge on the east, leading them to believe that he was hopelessly off the trail.

This ridge, he knew, joined the other at the point where Dora Crowell had shot the lion and from that point he foresaw little difficulty in finding the One Mile Creek Trail, where he purposed lying in wait for Kay and her abductors, for, long before, he had connected up the conversation that he had overheard in Bryam's shack the last night of the lion hunt, which fitted in so perfectly with all that had since transpired that he was now confident that it had related to the plan for Kay's abduction.

As Marvel drew up before the shack he called aloud to attract attention. The dogs had already come to meet him, but outside of this there were no signs of life about the place.

"I reckon they seen me and they all lit out," thought Marvel.

He dismounted; and as the dogs came to nose him, he petted the nearer of them, but all the while his eyes were on the ground; and from the trees on the hillside Bryam watched him, his vision interfered with by the foliage through which he looked.

"There's somethin' familiar about that son-of-a-gun," mused the watcher, "but I'll be danged if I can place him." Yet he hesitated to come out of hiding, and stood in silence while Bruce remounted and rode on up the canyon.

In the trampled earth in front of the cabin he had read a story that told him much. He had seen the fresh prints of horses hoofs and of the boots of men and among them the imprint of a small, high-heeled boot; and he knew that he was upon the right trail.

Just above the cabin, along the fresh trail of three horses, he came to a point where the spoor suddenly vanished. To one side lay a leafy branch freshly torn from a tree. The leaves at its lower end were frayed and dust covered; a shadow of a smile touched Marvel's lips.

"Punk work," he thought, as he rode on up the trail from which Bryam had brushed the signs of the passing of the three horsemen.

For a hundred feet the trail had been brushed clean of hoof prints and then they commenced again, as Marvel had known that they would. He rode on for another hundred yards until his eyes were attracted by something lying in the trail. Reining Baldy in, he leaned from his saddle and picked the thing up — a dainty handkerchief tied about a greasy playing card. For an instant he gazed at the tiny bit of linen; then, almost reverently, he tucked it inside his shirt. "Poor little kid," he murmured. "I wonder if you thought of me when you dropped this," and then he shook his head; "but, of course, you didn't for you don't know how much I love you."

At the point where the handkerchief and the card had been dropped, Marvel saw that the horsemen had turned abruptly to the right; and following their trail he came presently upon half of a torn playing card. "Paper chasin' has its advantages," he soliloquized. "It learns people tricks they might not have thought of." But here he did not need the evidence of the card.

The spoor lay plain before him, leading diagonally up the side of the ridge, back in the direction of the cabin.

With knitted brows, Bryam watched the rider,
and now for the first time he took particular note
of the horse. "Hell!" he muttered under his
breath. "That's that Baldy horse that the dude
rode."

The horse and rider were now in plain sight
upon the flank of the ridge; and something in the
way the man sat his horse, in the way he carried
his shoulders seemed familiar to Bryam; and
then, at last, he recognized him. "I'm a son-of-
a-gun," he ejaculated, "if it aint that nosey dude."

Bryam was worried. He was no intellectual
giant, but he had brains enough to see that Marvel was upon the trail of the girl and her abductors and to realize that the man knew that he
was on the right trail. Here was disaster. Here
was the end of his dream of affluence, to his share
of the ransom money; and here, too, was a man
who might definitely link him to the crime.

Bryam stepped from behind the trees that had
concealed him, and as he did so he cocked his
rifle. Throwing it to his shoulder, he took de-

liberate aim, while Marvel, guiding Baldy along the steep hillside, was concentrating his attention upon the spoor that he was following.

Bryam squeezed the trigger. A spurt of dust rose on the hillside on a level with Marvel's head; and with the simultaneous crack of the rifle, the man was electrified into instant action.

Almost as though he had been actuated by the same mechanism that released the hammer on Bryam's rifle, Marvel wheeled in his saddle, a forty-four ready in his hand.

Bryam was an excellent shot and so sure of himself that he could not have conceived that he might miss such an easy target; and so he had lowered his rifle after the first shot, certain of the result. Perhaps the clean miss disconcerted him, for he hesitated just an instant before he threw his rifle to his shoulder again for a second shot — a second shot that was never fired; for before he could align his sights, Marvel's old forty-four had spoken and Bryam, clutching at his breast, pitched forward upon his face.

For a moment Marvel sat watching his man to make sure that he was harmless; and then he reined on up the side of the ridge, turning constantly in the saddle to watch Bryam.

"He aint dead," he muttered, "but he sure is too sick to do any shootin'."

It was a hard pull to the summit, and he rested Baldy twice; but at last he rode into the more level trail along the top of the ridge and here another fragment of a playing card marked the way. At intervals he continued to find them; and always they brought a strange lump into his throat — these inarticulate appeals for help that the girl had left behind her.

"She's game," he murmured. "She sure is game, and she aint lost her head either."

He tried to figure how far ahead of him his quarry was, and from the signs along the trail he judged that it could not be more than five hours. His greatest fear and his greatest hope lay in Baldy. Their horses must have rested at Bryam's for several hours, but Baldy had had but two or three brief rests since the previous evening; yet he showed only the slightest indications of fatigue.

"I thought Bull's Eye was some horse, old boy," murmured Marvel, "but I guess you've got him faded, though," he added meditatively, "of course Bull's Eye never had nuthin' so important as this to travel for."

XVIii

On the Trail

MARVEL WAS far on the trail toward the south when the deputy sheriff and his posse rode up to Bryam's shack. The deputy was in the lead and the first thing that attracted his attention was four hounds that rose bristling and growling from about the body of a man a short distance up the side of the canyon to the left of the shack.

Riding quickly over to the prostrate man the deputy dismounted, while the hounds withdrew a short distance watching him suspiciously. He turned Bryam over on his back and saw that he still lived, though his shirt and the ground beneath him were soaked with blood.

The wounded man opened his eyes and looked up into the face of the deputy. Feebly he raised his hand and tried to point toward the east. "They," he gasped — "they headed for Deming over the east ridge."

Cory Blaine, who had been riding at the rear of the posse, rode up now and dismounted.

"Who shot you?" demanded the deputy.

With an effort that seemed to require all his remaining strength, Bryam answered, "That damned dude, Marvel." Then he saw Cory and beckoned to him to lean closer. "Send 'em away," he said. "I want to speak to you alone."

The deputy sheriff heard, but he hesitated.

"Let him speak to me alone," said Blaine. "I don't know what he wants, but I reckon it's about his family."

Withdrawing, the deputy motioned the other men away; and Cory knelt close and bent his ear close to Bryam's lips. "What is it, Hi?" he asked.

Bryam struggled and gasped. "He — ," blood

rushed from between his lips. He coughed and there was a rattling in his throat as he tried to speak again; then he sagged limply to the ground.

For a moment, squatting on his heels, Blaine looked at him; then he rose and turned toward the deputy. "He's done," he said.

"What did he tell you?" asked the officer, coming forward.

"He never got a chance to tell me nuthin'," said Cory. "He just died."

"Who's this guy Marvel he was tellin' about?" asked the deputy.

"He's the feller who rustled the girl," said Blaine.

"What makes you think that?" asked the officer.

"He was a guest up at my place and he got stuck on her. It got so bad that I kicked him out yesterday; but he must have had everything arranged, for he held me and the girl up and took her away from me. He knows her old man is rich and he's lookin' for the ransom. He can't be very far ahead of us because Bryam aint been shot long. The trail's hot now and you ought to pick him up before dark."

"Hell!" ejaculated the deputy. "There aint no trail over this here east ridge to Deming. That's the worst damn country anywhere about."

"So much the easier to get 'em," replied Blaine. "There's three of 'em; and they aint goin' to travel very fast — the girl can't stand it. If you start right now you ought to overhaul 'em before dark."

"There aint much use," said the deputy, "but we'll try it."

"I'll stay here and bury Hi," said Blaine, "and then I'll follow along and catch up with you."

"Come on, boys," called the deputy. "Water your horses and we'll get goin'."

As Cory Blaine watched the posse zig-zagging up the steep trail toward the summit of the east ridge, he was unquestionably worried. Uppermost in his mind was the question as to what Bruce Marvel had been doing here at Bryam's camp on the trail of Eddie and Mart. Who was the man? How had he got a start on all of them and what had led up to the gunfight between him and Bryam? As he tried to visualize all that had happened and the tragedy that had been enacted here at the head of Mill Creek Canyon, he reached the conclusion, from what Bryam had told the deputy sheriff, that his confederate had been successful in mis-directing Marvel onto the east trail; and by sending the sheriff and the posse after him, Bryam had given Eddie and Mart ample time in which to make good their escape into Sonora.

"Things aint turnin' out so bad after all," soliloquized Blaine. "This is just the break that I've been lookin' for."

He watched the riders picking their way up toward the summit of the ridge, but he did not move until the last of them had disappeared beyond the crest; then he swung quickly into his saddle and spurred up the trail toward the summit of the west ridge, leaving Hi Bryam lying where he died.

The sun was sinking in the west as Bruce Marvel started the descent upon the south side of the range. Below him lay a broad, desolate valley, and in the distance another range of mountains beyond which lay Mexico.

Level as a billiard table appeared the wide expanse of sage-dotted plain below him, but he well knew that it was a rough and rugged terrain cut by many washes. The trail that he was following descended along the summit of a hogback toward the distant valley. He paused for an instant upon this lofty shoulder of the range, his eyes searching far ahead in the hope that they might find a trace of the three riders who had preceded him. In the distance the outlines of another range of mountains lay purple against the sky, a low saddle marking the pass through which he knew the trail led onward into Sonora.

Far away he thought he discerned an indication of dust along the trail that the quarry would be following, and as he moved forward again his eyes dropped to a scrap of pasteboard lying on the ground ahead of him. It was half of a queen of hearts. Leaning from the saddle, he picked it up and tucked it in a pocket of his shirt. "Almost like gettin' a message from her," he soliloquized. "The queen of hearts — that would be a love letter. Shucks! I'm gettin' foolish in the head."

He rode on down an easy declevity, and twice again he thought he saw dust across the valley. Occasionally a fragment of a playing card appeared in the trail and it seemed to the lonely rider almost like talking to the girl who had dropped them.

Night was falling as he wound down the trail along the lower slopes of the mountains. His greatest immediate concern now was for Baldy. He had watered the horse in Mill Creek just above Bryam's cabin, but he had seen no signs of water out across the desolate, barren valley that he was entering; and Baldy had been traveling now for almost twenty hours with only a few brief rests. There was still a little grain left in the gunny sack at the cantle of his saddle, and once again he halted to rest and feed his mount and turn his blanket.

As yet the man himself felt neither hunger nor fatigue; and he knew that were it not for the shortage of water, both he and the horse could go on for many hours longer.

In the mountains across the valley there was water; and he determined to push on all night, if necessary, to reach it before the heat of a new day beat down upon them, taking its toll of moisture from their bodies.

While Baldy ate, Marvel examined the animal's feet and rubbed his legs; then he lay down

upon his back for a few minutes, seeking the re-
freshing rest of absolute relaxation.

"Everything was working out so pretty, Baldy.
It's too bad this had to happen," he said. "Another day or two at the most and it never could
have happened; but me and you will straighten
it out yet, old man." Baldy looked up from his
oats and gazed reflectively at the man. "I used
to think Bull's Eye was the best horse in the
world," said Marvel, "but I reckon he'll have to
take his hat off to you after this trip. Of course,
he never had no such chance as you. You got the
break, Baldy. I guess no other horse in the
world ever had such a break. You're goin' to be
a regular hero, Baldy — packin' me all them
miles to save the sweetest thing the sun ever shone
on."

It never occurred to Marvel that he might fail,
so sure was he of his horse and himself. It was
not egotism, but absolute self-confidence, coupled
with the knowledge that he must not fail, which
gave him this assurance.

"Well," he said presently, rising to his feet, "I
reckon we'd better be hittin' the trail. We've
loafed long enough."

He laid the blanket upon the horse's back, carefully smoothing out the wrinkles in the cloth; and then he lifted the heavy saddle from the ground. "Here's where one o' them postage stamps would come in handy," he remarked. "There really aint no sense in a horse packin' all this weight, which aint no use in a case like this."

Baldy appeared not even mildly interested in the relative merits of stock and English saddles. He grunted to the tightening of the forward cinch, and when he felt the rear cinch touch his belly he flattened his ears and reached back in that peculiar gesture of viciousness with which most horses indicate their disapproval of cinches in general and rear cinches in particular.

The trail lay dimly visible before him as Marvel turned Baldy's nose again toward the south; and presently it dropped into the mouth of a wide canyon, which it followed downward for a couple of miles. Crossing the canyon, which here turned toward the right, it rose abruptly again to higher ground.

Before the rider there lay once more the wide expanse of valley that now was but a black void,

rimmed upon the south by the black outlines of
the mountains, with the low saddle in the distance the only landmark to point the way.

"It's just like a great big black curtain turned
upside down," mused Marvel. "It hides everything and makes a fellow wonder what's behind
it. She's out there in it somewhere — I wish I
knew just where. She don't guess that I'm here;
and I reckon it wouldn't make any more difference to her if she did than as if it was Bud or some
other fellow; but it means a lot to me — it means
everything. I —— "

His soliloquy came to an abrupt stop, as far
away in the distance a point of light shone unexpectedly and mysteriously against the black
pall.

"That sure was an answer all right," he said,
"jumpin' up like that right when I was wishin'
I knew where she was. They sure must be crazy
to light a fire now, unless they think they got
such a start that no one can catch up to 'em anyway."

He was moving on again now and at the same
time endeavoring to restrain himself from urging Baldy to a faster gait; but his better judg-

ment prevailed, and he saved his horse at the expense of his own nerves, which chafed at the slow progress toward the goal which seemed now in sight.

For a great deal of the time the light was hidden when the trail dropped down onto lower ground and always then he feared that he might not see it again; but at intervals his view of it recurred and always it grew larger as he approached it until at last, just before the first streak of dawn had lighted the eastern sky, he topped a little rise of ground to see the fire in plain sight a few hundred yards away. It was burning low now — mostly a mass of glowing embers — and he could distinguish nothing in its vicinity.

He reined in his horse and dismounted quietly, praying that if this were indeed the camp he sought, the horses that he knew must be staked or hobbled nearby would not discover Baldy's presence and nicker a revealing welcome.

He led Baldy back along the trail to lower ground where the horse would be out of sight of the occupants of the camp, and tying him to a low bush, Marvel returned in the direction of the campfire. As he approached the higher ground from which it was visible, he dropped to his hands and knees and taking advantage of the bushes which dotted the ground, he crawled slowly forward. The stars had faded from the eastern sky, and the growing light of a new dawn was showing above the horizon.

Carefully the man crept forward. He could not afford to take the chance of premature discovery, for he was not sure just how many men he would have to face. He did not believe that Cory Blaine had been with the party at Bryam's shack, for he had seen the man ride out of camp that morning on a horse called Pudding Foot, which was remarkable for the roundness and size of his hoofs. The prints of Pudding Foot's feet he would have recognized, and he had seen no sign of them anywhere along the trail, but he did believe it possible that Blaine might have joined them later by another trail. So it was possible that he might have three desperate men to contend with instead of two; and then again there was the possibility that he would find no one about the campfire, at which they may have cooked some food and ridden on. With that thought came the first intimation of the nervous tension under which he had been laboring, for he broke into a cold sweat as he contemplated the possibility that, after all, he might not find Kay White here.

XIX

"STICK 'EM UP!"

NOW, AT last, he was within a few yards of the glowing embers, which were temporarily hidden from him by a low bush that had offered him concealment as he crawled forward. Removing his hat, he raised his head slowly until he could look over the top of the bush. In front of him, and now visible in the growing light of the new day, he saw a man sitting by the fire half reclining against a pile of saddles; and on the ground, beyond the fire, two forms were stretched.

Marvel replaced his hat upon his head and rose slowly, a forty-four in each hand. He advanced softly toward the man sleeping against the saddles; and now he was close enough to recognize that one of the other figures was that of a woman, and he breathed an almost audible sigh of relief. Beyond the camp he saw three horses standing patiently.

All this he took in in a single, brief glance; then he spoke.

"Stick 'em up!" he snapped sharply. "It's all over. I've got you covered."

Instantly the three awoke. "Stick 'em up!" snapped Marvel again, and the hands of the man by the saddle went quickly above his head; but the other man leaped to his feet and reached for his gun.

It all happened very quickly, so quickly that Kay White, awakened from a sleep of utter physical and nervous exhaustion, scarcely realized that she had seen a man killed. Sharp words had awakened her, and as she opened her eyes she had seen a sudden streak of fire accompanied by the bellow of a forty-four; and then the man that she had heard called Mart had pitched forward upon his face and lain very still, his body almost touching her feet.

"Get up," said the killer to the man against the saddles, "and keep 'em up. Face the other way."

There was a note in the man's voice that was familiar to the girl, but she knew at once that it was not Cory Blaine. Only once before had she heard Marvel speak with a tone of authority; and then his voice had not been hardened by long suppressed hate and anger; so she recognized only a strange familiarity, while his clothes meant nothing to her since she had never seen him dressed thus before, and it was not yet light enough to distinguish his features. She saw him slip one of his own guns into its holster and remove the weapon from Eddie's holster. Then he turned to her.

"You all right, Kay?" he asked. "They aint hurt you none, have they?" And with the sudden change in his tone, she recognized him.

"Bruce!" she exclaimed. "I —" A sob choked other words in her throat.

"You're all right now, Kay," he said. "There can't nuthin' happen to you now. Your papa is at the ranch, and we'll have you back there in no time. But tell me first, did either of these men harm you? If they did, I'm goin' to kill this one now. I aint goin' to take no chances with the law. It lets too many of them escape."

"I never done nuthin' to her," said the man in a voice that was barely articulate, so muffled was it by some impediment of speech.

"No," said Kay. "They treated me all right, especially Eddie. That is Eddie there," she explained, indicating the man standing before Marvel.

"Yes," said Marvel. "I know Eddie. I've been lookin' for him for a long time."

"Who the hell are you?" demanded Eddie. "I never seen you before."

"And that wise guy, who thought he could beat me to the draw after I drawed, would be Mart, wouldn't he?" demanded Marvel.

"Who are you anyway?" demanded Eddie.

"It wouldn't do you no good to know now, son," replied Marvel. "When you should have known who I was was a couple of days ago." He stepped quickly over to Mart and, stooping, recovered the gun that had dropped from the man's hand when he fell and also extricated the other from its holster.   Then he laid all four weapons beside Kay. "Watch 'em," he said. "That feller may not be dead.   I aint got time to examine him now."   He turned to Eddie.   "Take a tie rope off o' one of them saddles," he said, and when the man had done as he was bid, Marvel secured his wrists behind him.

Kay White sat in bewildered silence, partially overcome by the sudden turn in her fortune and partially by her surprise at seeing Marvel in this new role.   Here was no man playing a part, and she realized that for the first time she was looking upon the real Bruce Marvel.   She noted his clothes as the light increased and how much a part of him they seemed.   She recalled the doubt that she had felt concerning him, and she wanted to say something to him.   She wanted to explain and to ask his forgiveness, but she did not know how to say it; so she remained silent.

"Got any grub in camp, Eddie?" asked Marvel. "I aint eat for so long I've forgotten what it's like."

"There's food in a couple of them bags," said Eddie sullenly, pointing to the pile of saddles.

Marvel searched among the bags.   In one he

found a frying pan, a coffee pot and some tin cups, and in another bacon, potatoes and a can of coffee, in addition to which there were three canteens, one of which was full and another that had some water in it.

"I reckon this'll do," he said. "Hungry, Kay?"

"Not very," she replied.

"Well, you better eat," he said. "We got a long pull ahead of us yet and you've got to keep your strength."

He busied himself preparing their frugal meal and when it was ready, he served Kay, after which he freed Eddie's hands that he, too, might eat.

While he ate Marvel squatted on his heels directly in front of Eddie. "Where's Blaine?" he demanded suddenly.

"He —" Eddie hesitated. "How the hell do I know where he is?"

"Listen, Eddie, I know all about you," said Marvel. "Come clean and it may go easier with you. I think you're expectin' Blaine. I want to know when you expect him and what trail he's comin' on. If you don't answer me, or if you lie to me, and Blaine comes on us unexpected, I'm goin' to shoot you first."

"He's comin' the same trail we come on," replied Eddie after considerable hesitation. "He didn't aim on catchin' up to us until after we reached —" He stopped.

"Until after you reached Kelly's place in Sonora," suggested Marvel.

"If you know so much what's the use of askin' me?" demanded Eddie.

"There aint none," replied Marvel; "but we're goin' back to the TF by a different trail, and if we meet Blaine on that trail you can kiss yourself good-bye. I don't want no unexpected or promiscuous shootin' while I got Miss White with me."

"There aint no other trail to the TF, least ways no shorter one."

"Oh, yes, they is," said Marvel. "When I was a kid I helped my old man trail some cattle up from the border this a-way; so I know there's another trail and besides that, there's water on it."

Eddie contemplated Marvel for a moment. "You must be the guy that planted all the willows on the cricks in this part of the country," he said; "but it's funny I never seen you before."

"I told you once that you have seen me before. You saw me day before yesterday."

A sudden light of recognition dawned in Eddie's eyes. "Why you're that damn dude," he said.

The shadow of a smile moved Marvel's lips. "We'll be movin' now," he said, and then he turned toward the girl. "It's mighty hard on you, Kay, but I don't see no way out of it. We couldn't stay here in a dry camp nohow, and then particularly I don't want no rumpus with Blaine while you are with us."

"Don't think of me," she said. "Do whatever you believe the right thing to do. I'm tired, of course, but I'm very far from being exhausted."

"You're sure a wonder, Kay," he said admiringly, as he busied himself with the rope with which he was again securing Eddie's wrists. Then he removed Eddie's cartridge belt from about the man's hips and handed it to Kay. "Strap this on," he said, "and take one of those forty-fives. I hope you won't need it, but I'll feel safer if you have it."

As she followed his instructions, he walked out
and brought in the three horses, which she held
while he saddled and bridled them.

"Where is your horse?" she asked.

"I hid him over yonder," he replied. "We'll
pick him up on our way out."

"What are you going to do with him?" She
nodded her head toward Mart's body.

"I can't do nuthin' with him," replied Marvel.
"We aint got nuthin' to dig a hole with and we
aint got time if we had. I might pack him in on
his horse, but we may need the horse. One of
our's might give out."

"You are just going to leave him lying there?"
she asked incredulously.

"There aint no other way, Kay," he replied;
"and even that is too good for him." His tone
was as hard as his words, for they reflected the
contempt that he held for the dead man.

She said no more, but mounted Lightfoot and
turned her back upon the body of the dead Mart.
Marvel assisted Eddie into the saddle; and then
he mounted Mart's horse, and the three rode to
where Baldy was tied.

"I reckon I'll give you a rest, old man," he

said, and handing the lead rope to Kay, he remounted. "I'll lead Eddie's horse," he said, "and
you follow with Baldy. It's been a long time
since I've been over this trail, but if I remember
right there's water in the next ten or fifteen
miles."

Since the unexpected arrival of Marvel and
the rapid and grim sequence of events that had
followed, Kay White had scarcely spoken. Perhaps the shock to her nervous system, already
weakened by fatigue, had left her dazed; but now
as she rode along the trail in the rear of Marvel
and Eddie she had time to reveiw the happen-
ings of the past hour. Uppermost in her mind,
naturally, was the killing of Mart. Never before
had she witnessed tragedy at such close range;
and she was impressed more by the horror of the
casualness of it, perhaps, than she was by the
death itself. It seemed to her that a man who
might have been forced to shoot a dog would
have evidenced more feeling in the matter than
Marvel had.

She almost shrank from the thought of being
near him; and then she realized that this was but
a natural reaction, resulting from emotional com-

plexes rather than from studied and rational consideration of the events leading up to the deed. Then came the realization that what he had done had been for her and she was filled with remorse for the unjust thoughts she had harbored.

Eddie rode in sullen silence, his weak and stupid face a study of hopeless dejection. He knew nothing of the legal penalty for kidnaping; but he was conversant with the rough and ready justice of his fellow men, which raised within his mind the vision of a lonely figure suspended from a tree. He did not like the picture. It gave him a most uncomfortable sensation about the neck, and so his mind groped muddily for a plan to escape.

Marvel, constantly alert, rode in the lead. Occasionally he turned in his saddle and scanned the country for signs of pursuit. He was very happy; and by way of expression he hummed snatches of a little song that was more notable for its doleful lugubriousness than for any intrinsic value it possessed as a work of art; and thus, each occupied with his own thoughts, the three followed the dim trail toward the north.

XX

WATER!

BLAINE, MOUNTED upon a comparatively fresh horse, made good time along the trail from Bryam's shack toward the south. Before darkness had fallen the preceding day to obliterate all signs along the way, two features of the spoor had puzzled him. Fragments of torn playing cards appeared so often in the trail as to convince him that someone had been blazing it for a purpose and he could only assume, as had Marvel, that it was the girl. The other was not quite so

plain, but he thought that it indicated that four
horsemen instead of three had preceded him.
His trailing ability, however, was not so great
that he could be positive of this, nor did the signs
tell him that three of the horsemen had preceded
the fourth by several hours.

So sure was he, however, that Bryam had mis-
directed Marvel toward the east that he succeeded in almost convincing himself that he was
in error in believing that four horses recently
had passed along the trail.

With the coming of the new day he saw that
the spoor had been dimmed and in some places
obliterated by the footprints of nocturnal animals
which, by night, follow man-made paths, the
open, dusty parts of which are the plazas of the
little folk where they come to stroll and to play.

But for such things Blaine had neither eyes nor
thoughts as he strained the former far into the
distance ahead in search of some tell-tale moving
thing that might indicate the whereabouts of
those whom he sought.

"If Marvel did follow 'em and caught up with
'em," he soliloquized, "the boys sure must have
bumped him off; but if he got the drop on 'em

he would be coming back this way, and I ought to be meeting him pretty soon." He loosened the gun in its holster and redoubled his alertness. "It aint that I'm afraid of the damn dude," he apologized to himself, "but he might be lyin' in wait for me behind some bush — him and his funny panties. If I ever get the chance I'm goin' to shoot them panties full of holes, more especially if he's in 'em."

The trail dropped into a hollow and then rose again to higher ground, and as he topped this rise he saw something just ahead that brought him to a sudden stop and his gun from its holster — it was the figure of a man lying beside the ashes of a fire.

The instant that he saw it he knew that the man was dead. At first he thought it was Marvel because he hoped that it was; but as he rode closer, after convincing himself that there was no one around, he saw that if was Mart; and he cursed beneath his breath.

Dismounting beside the dead man he turned him over on his back. For a moment he stood looking at him. "Dead as a door nail," he muttered. Then he stooped and ran his hand inside the dead man's shirt. "He aint plumb cold yet," he soliloquized. "That means whoever done this aint far off."

Searching the ground he found the spoor of three horses leading away from the camp. At a short distance farther on, where Marvel had left his horse, he counted the tracks of four horses leading to the north. Nowhere ahead could he see any sign of horsemen.

"If it's that damn dude," he said, "he's lost himself, which will give me a chance to get back to the TF ahead of him. Then it'll be his word against mine." For a few minutes he sat there puzzling out his problem, and then the light of a sudden inspiration was reflected in his eyes. "No," he said, half aloud, "it will be better than my word against his. It'll be mine and Bryam's and Mart's. The three of us together ought to be able to put a rope around that bozo's neck."

Blaine was a hard rider. He never gave any thought to his horse, nor to the future, but only to the present necessity for speed; and now he wheeled his mount and spurred back along the trail he had come, bent only on reaching the TF Ranch ahead of Marvel and praying as he rode that it was indeed Marvel who had overtaken his two confederates and presumably rescued Kay White. He knew that his horse would hold out at least as far as Bryam's; and there he could change to Bryam's horse, which he had seen hobbled and grazing in the vicinity of the cabin; so he had no doubts but that he could reach the ranch long in advance of Marvel, even though the other was not lost as he believed and was able to find his way back to the TF without delay.

Marvel, pushing along the dim trail, was acutely aware that their horses were commencing to weaken from fatigue and thirst under the heat of the burning sun. He no longer hummed his sad little tune, for he was genuinely worried, harassed as he was by the haunting fear that the spring where his father had camped years before might since have gone dry, or that he might miss it entirely.

Perhaps he had staked too much upon his ability to find that waterhole. If their horses gave out and they were left afoot in that arid waste, their situation might indeed be hopeless. He was not thinking of himself or of the other man, but only of the girl. He reproached himself for having taken this long chance, yet when he considered the fact that the girl must inevitably have had to face the dangers of a gun battle with Blaine had they returned by the other trail, he still thought that his decision had been a wise one, and once again his self confidence asserted itself and he became strong again in the conviction that they would find water soon.

His train of thought and the long silence were broken by Eddie. "This horse of mine aint goin' much further," he said. "He is about through."

Marvel turned in his saddle. For some time he had had to drag the other horse along with a couple of turns of his rope about the horn of his saddle and now he saw that the beast was staggering and weak.

He reined in. "We'll switch you over to this horse," he said, "and I'll ride Baldy. How's your horse comin', Kay?"

"He seems to be holding up pretty well," she replied. "He hasn't the weight to carry that the others have."

"You better get back on the other trail to Bryam's where we can get water," growled Eddie. "There aint no water here."

"Shut up," admonished Marvel, "and speak when you're spoken to."

Dismounting, they rested their horses for several minutes. Marvel considered the advisability of abandoning Eddie's horse, but finally decided to take him on as far as he could go, for he knew that if he could get him to water and rest there for a couple of hours the animal might recuperate sufficiently to prove useful to them before their long ride was over.

Shortly after they took up the march again, Baldy lifted his nose in the air and pricked up his ears and almost immediately the other horses did the same, the four of them pushing suddenly forward with accelerated speed. Marvel breathed a sigh of relief.

"What's the matter with the horses?" called Kay from her position in the rear. "They act as though they saw something."

"They smell water," replied Marvel, "and it makes them feel good; but take it from me it don't make them feel half as good as it does me."

The horses moved forward eagerly now and with vitality renewed by anticipation of the opportunity of quenching their thirst in the near future. The change in the spirits of their mounts seemed also to revivify the riders; so that it was with much lighter hearts that the three rode on beneath the pitiless rays of an Arizona sun, Marvel giving Baldy his head in the knowledge that the animal's instinct would lead it unerringly to the nearest water.

Ahead of them stretched what appeared to be an unbroken expanse of rolling brush land, lying arid and uninviting in the shimmering heat of the morning.

Presently there broke upon Marvel's vision the scene for which he had been waiting, the picture of which he had been carrying in his memory since boyhood — a large, bowl-like depression, in the bottom of which green verdue proclaimed the presence of the element that might mean the difference between life and death to them.

As they dropped over the edge and rode down a steep trail leading toward the water, Eddie contemplated the back of the man riding just ahead of him. "Dude!" he murmured. "I wonder what long-eared, locoed son-of-a-gun hitched that monicker onto this bozo?"

"You speakin' to me, young feller?" asked

Marvel, for the mutterings of the man had come to his ears, although he had not been able to interpret the meaning.

"You and your old man trailed cattle this a-way when you were a kid?" asked Eddie.

"Yes."

"What made 'em think you were a dude?" demanded the man.

"Who said I was a dude?" asked Marvel.

"Butts —" Eddie stopped in confusion.

"So you know Butts, too, eh?" asked Marvel, casually.

Eddie hesitated. "I seen him once," he said at last.

"Don't worry, Eddie," said Marvel. "You aint give nuthin' away. As I told you once before I know all about you — all five of you."

"You think you're a smart guy," said Eddie, "but you aint got nuthin' on me. They aint no law against my knowin' people."

"It aint so good for your health to know some folks too well, though, Eddie," replied Bruce. "I can think of three of 'em offhand right now — there used to be five, but two of 'em's dead."

Eddie looked up quickly from contemplation

of his saddle horn.   He thought a moment.
"Who's the other?" he asked.

"Bryam," replied Marvel.

"Did you kill him?"

"I had to, Eddie. He was shootin' at me with
a thirty-thirty, and for a lion hunter I will say
that he was a damn poor shot." It went against
Marvel's grain to speak of this killing, much less
to boast of it; but for reasons of his own he
wished to break down the man's morale — in the
vernacular, to put the fear of God into him —
and he knew that if Eddie had Bryam to think of
now as well as Mart, he would worry that much
more over his own possible fate and break the
easier under the strain when the time came.

The balance of the trail into the bottom of the
depression they negotiated in silence.   Marvel
noted with relief that green grass grew over a
considerable area around the spring.   He had
not even dared hope for such good fortune as
this.

"They can't be runnin' many cattle in here
this year," he said to Eddie.

"They aint never run nuthin' in here since I've
been in this neck of the woods," replied Eddie,

"and I aint never even been in this valley before. They aint near as many cattle on the range as they used to be since the cattle business got bumped a few years ago, and there still bein' some rustlin' over the border, no one ranges in here no more."

"The feed never was no good in this valley anyhow, I guess," said Marvel. "They used to feed in the hills on both sides and water in this hole on the way across."

They halted beside a spring of clear, cold water that ran a little stream for a hundred yards or so before it sank into the earth again. Below the main spring they watered their horses, permitting them only a little at a time. Marvel took a half hour to this, releasing Eddie's hands that he might assist him, while Kay filled their canteens and each of them quenched his thirst. After the two men had hobbled their horses and turned them loose, Marvel secured Eddie's wrists again; then the three threw themselves upon the ground to rest.

Bruce made Kay lie at full length and relax, and he wet his bandana and brought it and laid it across her forehead. Eddie needed no invita-

tion to lie down, though he grumbled at the uncomfortable position his bound wrists necessi-
tated. Marvel lay where he could watch the trail
down which they had come into the depression
and where, at the same time, he could watch the
horses, for he knew that they might be the first
to give warning of the approach of a pursuer.
Occasionally the man turned his head and looked
at the girl lying quietly a few yards away. How
soft and small she looked; and always the sight
induced a strange sensation in his breast — a sudden fullness. "By golly," he soliloquized, "it's
just like I wanted to cry; but I don't want to cry,
I want to sing. There's something about her that
makes a fellow want to sing when he's close to
her."

Presently he saw by the steady rising and falling of her breasts that she had fallen asleep. He
half rose then and hitched himself over close to
where Eddie lay. The man looked up at him.
"I want to talk to you, young fellow," he said;
and then, in a low tone that might not awaken
the girl, he talked steadily for several minutes,
while the changing expressions upon the face of
his listener denoted various reactions, the most

marked of which were surprise, consternation, and fear.

"I aint askin' you nuthin'," he said in conclusion. "There aint nuthin' to ask you, I just been tellin' you. Now if you know what's good for you, you'll know how to act." As he ceased speaking he drew a large pocket knife from his overalls and opened one of the blades. Then he drew one of his forty-fours, the wooden grip of which bore many notches, the edges of which were rounded and smooth and polished by the use of many years. As Eddie watched him, fascinated, Marvel cut two new notches below the older ones.

"Them's Bryam and Mart?" asked the prisoner.

Marvel nodded. "And there's room for some more yet, Eddie," he said.

"You make all them?" asked Eddie.

"No," replied Marvel. "These guns were my father's."

"He must have been a bad man from way back," commented Eddie in frank admiration.

"He weren't nuthin' of the kind," replied Bruce. "He was a sheriff."

"Oh!" said Eddie.

For two hours they rested there; and while they rested, Cory Blaine drove his faltering mount ruthlessly along the back trail toward Bryam's.

They had had several hours start of him, but their rest and the killing pace that he was travelling might easily permit him to overcome the handicap; so that now it was a race with, perhaps, much depending upon who reached the TF Ranch first, though only Cory Blaine realized that it was a race.

For two hours Marvel permitted the girl and the horses to rest and recuperate. Then he aroused Eddie, removed his bonds and the two men went out and fetched the horses back to the spring. Not until they were saddled and ready to ride did he arouse Kay.

"I hate to do it," he said, as she opened her eyes to the pressure of his hand upon her shoulder, "but we got to get goin'. We can't make the ranch tonight, but if the horses hold out we ought to pull in some time after breakfast in the mornin'."

xxi

"He Is Buck Mason"

As they mounted and rode away, Cory Blaine was looking down upon Bryam's shack from the summit of the ridge near the head of Mill Creek Canyon. His horse, blowing and trembling, faltered at the edge of the steep trail pitching down into the canyon. As Blaine urged him forward, the animal took a few faltering steps, then he swayed and dropped in his tracks.

"Hell!" muttered Blaine. "Now I got to hoof it to the bottom and pack my saddle to boot."

Trudging down the steep trail beneath the weight of his heavy saddle, he caught occasional glimpses of Bryam's body lying where he had left it. Above, on ragged wings, great black birds swung in easy, majestic circles. Occasionally one of them would swoop lower; but four bristling, growling hounds kept them at bay.

In the shade of a tree near the shack, Bryam's hobbled horse stood patiently, switching his tail in perpetual battle with the flies, while he rested in the shade during the heat of the day before going out to graze again on the meadowland below the shack.

Two of the hounds came menacingly toward Blaine as he approached; but he circled them; and when they saw that he was not coming nearer to their dead master, they stopped and stood watching him as he saddled and bridled the horse, removed its hobbles and rode away down the valley.

The guests of the TF Ranch were at breakfast when Cory Blaine rode into the corral and unsaddled. No one had seen him arrive, and he went directly to the bunkhouse. When he entered he saw Butts just pulling on his boots, the other men having already gone to their breakfast.

The two men eyed one another. "Did you get the girl?" demanded Butts.

"Hell, no," replied Blaine.

"Where is she?"

"That damn dude beat me to it," replied Blaine. "He got her."

"You don't mean that Marvel feller?" demanded Butts.

"Yes."

"You seen him and didn't plug him?"

"I didn't see him."

"Then how do you know he got the girl?" asked Butts.

"He killed Bryam."

"The hell you say."

"Yes. And Hi lived long enough just to tell who killed him. Then I followed the dude's trail to where he come up with Eddie and Mart and the girl."

"He took her away from them?" asked Butts.

"He plugged Mart; and I reckon he got the drop on Eddie, for I seen where the three of 'em rode off; but they took the wrong trail, and I reckon they're lost somewhere in the hills."

Butts looked worried. "They may be lost," he said, "and they may not; but they'll get here sometime, and when they do here's one bozo's goin' to be missin', and you better come with me."

"Don't be a fool, Butts," replied Blaine. "When they hear my story they won't never hang it on us. I got it all figured out; and, believe me, that fellow Marvel is goin' to swing for the murder of Bryam and Mart, to say nuthin' of what he'll get for abductin' the girl."

"You sure you can do it, Cory?" asked Butts.

"I know I can. You come along with me now. I'm goin' up to the house and give 'em some facts that'll make their eyes pop out. I aint killed one horse and damn near killed another to get here ahead of Marvel for nuthin'."

"All right," said Butts, "but I'd feel a whole lot safer if I was headin' for somewhere's else."

"That'll be just like tellin' 'em you was guilty," said Blaine.

The two men approached the veranda of the big house just as the guests were coming out from breakfast.

"There's Cory!" exclaimed Dora Crowell.

John White stepped forward as the two men came up the steps. "Have you any news, Blaine?" he asked.

"A lot of it, sir," replied Cory. The other guests clustered about, eager and attentive.

"Tell me what you know," said White.

"I trailed the abductors as far as Bryam's cabin. They was three of 'em. I guess Hi must have tried to interfere with 'em, because Marvel shot him."

"Marvel!" exclaimed two or three of them simultaneously.

"Yes, Marvel," replied Blaine. "I was always afraid of that fellow. That's why I kicked him out. I knew right along that he was after Kay."

"How do you know it was Marvel?" demanded Dora Crowell.

"Hi told me just before he died. The deputy sheriff and the posse were there at the same time. They heard him. Then the posse rode one way and I rode the other, lookin' for trails; and I found their trail leadin' down toward Sonora. I rode all night, and in the mornin' I came on their camp. They weren't no one there except one feller who was shot through the chest. He was still livin', and he told me how it happened.

"He said his name was Mart and that he and another guy had been hired by Marvel to work for him, but he hadn't let 'em in on what he was goin' to do till the last minute. When they got to this camp this feller Mart said he wouldn't have nuthin' more to do with it. He told Marvel he was goin' to quit and go back, and the other feller wanted to quit, too; and then Marvel shot this feller Mart.

"He said he was unconscious for a long time and didn't know what happened after he was shot. He didn't know whether Marvel killed the other feller, too, or made a prisoner of him, or finally persuaded him to come along with him; but before the shootin' Marvel said he was goin' right back and claim the reward. He even got Kay to promise not to accuse him by threatening to kill her and her father if she did. I tell you he's a bad one, and he's comin' in here with a story of how he rescued Kay. I tell you it was a lucky thing I come on that Mart when I did."

"What happened to him?" asked Dora. "Where is he?"

"He died right after he told his story to me," replied Cory.

"One would have thought that such a desperado would have made sure that both his victims were dead before he left them," said Dora.

"I reckon he thought they was dead," said Blaine.

"What do you suppose has become of the posse?" asked White. "Could it be possible that they may have overhauled Marvel?"

"No," replied Blaine. "They went in a different direction. Aint they back yet?"

"No. I wish that some of them might be here when Marvel came in, so that they could make the arrest, but the sheriff is back from his trip and I'll telephone him at once."

"I reckon you better do that," said Blaine.

"I just can't believe it," said Birdie Talbot as White stepped into the house to telephone. "Bruce was such a nice young man."

"It just doesn't seem possible," said Miss Pruell. "It doesn't seem possible at all."

"I aint surprised," said Butts. "I always said there was somethin' phoney about that bozo, but I don't see how he ever killed anyone with a gun.

He must have snuck up on 'em while they was asleep, or maybe when they seen his panties they committed suicide."

"I don't know nuthin' about that," said Blaine, "but he sure is one bad hombre."

"I don't believe a word of it," said Dora Crowell, looking Blaine steadily in the eye.

The man flushed. "It's a good thing for you you're not a man," said Blaine.

"Perhaps it's a better thing for you that I am not, Cory," she replied.

Blaine turned away. "I aint goin' to stay here jawin' with no fool woman," he said. "I aint had no sleep for two nights; and I'm goin' to turn in," and with Butts at his side he walked back toward the bunkhouse.

After the two men had left them, the guests fell into a discussion of Blaine's charges against Marvel. Some agreed with Dora, while others took sides with Blaine. Miss Pruell reiterated that she just couldn't believe such a thing about Mr. Marvel.

"I guess he must be guilty," said Birdie Talbot, "after all that Cory has told us. We have known Cory much longer than we have Marvel, and there is no reason why we should not believe him. You know I always did suspect something funny about Marvel. I suspicioned him right away when he kept refusing to play bridge."

Benson Talbot, running true to form, took sides against his wife.

"It looks pretty bad for Marvel," said Bert Adams, "and perhaps it seems worse to some of us because we know that he was not what he pretended to be. But there was something else about him that the rest of you don't seem to recall that comes pretty nearly convincing me that he is guilty of all that Blaine accuses him of."

"What's that?" demanded Benson Talbot.

"His eyes," replied Adams.

"Why I think he has nice eyes," said Miss Pruell.

"He has the eyes of a killer," stated Adams confidently.

"Slush!" exclaimed Dora Crowell.

Olga Gunderstrom had not entered into the discussion because she knew nothing of either Marvel or Blaine. In fact, the whole matter seemed to bore her and now she turned away. "I am going to my room, Dora," she said. "I think

I shall lie down for a few moments." And then, one by one, the guests drifted into the house to read or write letters or to rest, so that the veranda was deserted when Bruce and Kay and Eddie rode into the ranch yard.

Marvel led them to the foot of the veranda steps, and when they had dismounted he told Kay that she had better go to her room immediately and get some rest. "I reckon the reason there's nobody about is that they are all out lookin' for you," he said, but even as he spoke John White stepped out onto the veranda. As father and daughter saw one another they rushed into each other's arms. There were tears in the man's eyes, while Kay sobbed openly.

"You are all right, darling?" he asked.

"All right, dad," she replied through her sobs, "and we have no one to thank for that but Bruce — Mr. Marvel."

The older man's face hardened, but the girl did not see it for hers was buried upon his shoulder. "I know all about that, dear," he said. "Now you go to your room and get some rest and I will talk with Mr. Marvel."

She turned and smiled through her tears at

Bruce. "I haven't thanked you yet," she said, "but sometime I am going to try."

"Never you mind the thanks," he said; "you get to bed."

When she had gone, White descended the veranda steps and faced Marvel. "Blaine is back," he said.

"I reckoned as much," said Marvel. "Where is he?"

"He told the whole story," said White. "I ought to kill you, Marvel; but you brought her back unharmed, and I owe you something for that. I am going to give you a chance to get away. The sheriff is on his way here now. You get on yours and I'll tell him that I do not intend to prosecute."

Marvel looked at the older man for a moment. "I sure would have known that Blaine was back," he said, "even if you hadn't told me. I aint goin' to try to tell you nuthin', Mr. White, except that you are all wrong. I thank you for what you think you're tryin' to do for me, but I'm not goin' away. Kay knows the truth, and you will know it after you have listened to her. I had nuthin' to do with her abduction."

"It's no use, Marvel," replied White. "Blaine's story was too circumstantial."

Olga Gunderstrom came onto the veranda as Marvel shook his head and was about to turn away. As their eyes met the girl stopped and hers went wide. "Buck Mason!" she exclaimed.

"Olga!" cried the man, and started up the steps toward her.

"Don't come near me, you murderer," she cried.

"I had to shoot 'em both in self defense, Olga," he said. "Bryam was shootin' at me with a thirty-thirty and the other feller tried to draw after I had him covered."

"I don't mean those two," she said. "You know who I mean."

"Olga!" he cried. "I couldn't guess that you'd believe that about me. I heard that story, too; but I knew that you would know that I never done it."

She shuddered. "I know your kind," she said icily; "no refinement, no instincts of decency, just a common brute, who can think of nothing else but to kill."

He looked at her in bitter silence for a long moment. Pain, disillusionment, sorrow made a raging chaos of his brain; but at last the only outward expression of what was passing within was the reflection of the sorrow that lay deep in his eyes. Then he turned away, hesitated and turned back toward John White.

"I'll turn this feller over to you, sir," he said, indicating Eddie with a gesture. "Hold him until the sheriff comes."

"I told you I was not going to prosecute," said White.

"But I am," said Mason. "I am a deputy sheriff and I deputize you to take custody of this prisoner;" and then he turned and walked away, leading the four horses toward the corral.

"Don't let him get away, Mr. White," cried Olga. "Do something. Don't let him get away."

"What can I do?" asked White with a shrug. "He is a known killer; and he's carrying two guns, while I am unarmed."

In her room Kay White was troubled. There had been something in the way that her father had listened to her praise of Marvel that had seemed cold and austere. Perhaps it was a woman's intuition that all was not right that brought

her out onto the veranda while Olga was plead-
ing with her father.

"I tell you something must be done," cried
Olga. "He must not be permitted to escape."

"I have telephoned the sheriff," replied White.
"He is on his way here now."

"That will be too late," replied the girl. "He
may get away, and then we may never be able to
catch him again."

"Who?" demanded Kay. "Who may get
away?"

"Buck Mason, the murderer of my father," replied Olga.

"Buck Mason!" exclaimed Kay. "Who is he?"

White pointed toward Marvel who was leading the horses into the corral. "He is Buck Mason," he replied.

XXII

"You're Under Arrest"

Kay White stood for a moment looking at the man unsaddling the horses in the corral. "Buck Mason," she murmured, and then turning to Olga, "He may be Buck Mason," she said; "but no one can ever make me believe that he is a murderer."

"It is immaterial to me what you believe," snapped Olga; "and if your father won't arrest him, Cory Blaine will." As she spoke she started down the veranda steps and walked rapidly toward the bunkhouse.

Kay White followed her. "Don't," she cried. "You don't know what you are doing. They will kill him. They want to kill him. All they want is the excuse."

"I pray to God that they will kill him," said Olga, "for he killed my father."

As Olga hurried on toward the bunkhouse, Kay White broke into a run and, passing her, hastened to the corral, where Mason was just turning the horses into pasture. As he fastened the gate and turned back he saw her.

"I thought I told you to go to bed," he said.

"Oh, Bruce," she cried. "Hurry and get away from here. That girl, I suppose she is Miss Gunderstrom from what she said, has gone to get Cory Blaine to arrest you."

"Why should I run away, Kay?" he asked. "Don't tell me that you think I done it."

"Oh, I don't care whether you did or not. I don't want them to kill you, and I know that they will kill you. They won't give you a chance, Bruce."

"It's worth being killed a dozen times for, Kay, to hear you say that," he said; "but don't you worry. You get back to the house quick in case there's goin' to be any shootin'. I can take care of myself, now that you've warned me."

Breathlessly, Olga Gunderstrom broke into the bunkhouse. Butts was sitting on the edge of his bunk rolling a cigarette, and Blaine was already stretched out on his asleep.

"Buck Mason is here," she cried, "the man who murdered my father." Blaine sat up on his bunk.

"What's that?" he demanded.

"The man who murdered my father is here," she cried, "and there's five thousand dollare reward for him dead or alive."

"Where is he?" demanded Blaine, leaping to his feet.

The girl pointed through the window to the corral. "There he is," she said.

The two men looked. "My God!" exclaimed Butts. "If it aint the damn dude."

The two men hastily buckled on their cartridge belts and guns. "You beat it back to the house in a hurry, Miss," said Blaine.

"Be careful," said Olga. "He's a dangerous character."

"Shucks," scoffed Butts, as the girl left the bunkhouse and hastened toward the ranch house, "that dude couldn't even hit a tree at fifty feet."

Kay White reached the house a moment after Olga. "What did you do? Did you warn him?" demanded the latter.

"Of course I did," replied Kay.

"Then you ought to be killed, too," cried Olga. "You are as bad as the murderer."

John White, hearing the girls' voices, came from the office where he had deposited Eddie and taken the further precaution of binding the man's ankles together. "Come, Kay," he said. "You girls are both nervous and distraught. Please go to your rooms, both of you. If they try to take Marvel, or Mason, or whatever his name is, there will unquestionably be shooting and it will not be safe for you out here."

Olga was pacing up and down the veranda like a caged tigress as Kay entered the house and went to her room. In the doorway she turned. "I wish that you would come with me, father," she said. "You must listen to me. You must know the truth." And then suddenly, "Where is Eddie?"

"Eddie! Who is Eddie?" demanded White. "You mean the prisoner?"

"Yes."

"He's tied up as tight as a Scotchman's purse-strings and stowed away in the office," replied her father, as he followed Kay to her room.

Eddie, sitting upon a chair in the office, saw Olga pacing up and down the veranda, back and forth past the office window. He had heard the girl accuse Marvel as the murderer of her father. He had heard her call him Buck Mason; and now a faint light burst upon his dull intellect, so that he understood much that he had not understood before. He saw not only the immediate necessity for escape but something that held out a hope for its accomplishment; and so as Olga approached the office window again, he hailed her.

"Hey, Miss," he cried.

The girl stopped and looked into the office. "What do you want?" she asked.

"Let me loose," he said, "and I'll help Blaine and Butts get that fellow, Mason. I got it in for him myself, and two of 'em aint enough."

She hesitated. "Why not?" she thought, for her mind was obsessed only with revenge. She stepped quickly into the office and, after some difficulty, untied the knot that secured Eddie's wrists. His hands free, the man quickly loosened the cords about his ankles. Then he sprang through the doorway, vaulted over the rail and started diagonally across the valley toward the hills on the opposite side.

"Come back!" cried Olga Gunderstrom. "You are going the wrong way."

"The hell I am," said Eddie, bursting into a new spurt of speed.

From the corral Buck Mason had watched Kay White until she reached the safety of the house. Then he stepped inside the stables. He withdrew his guns from their holsters one at a time and examined them carefully. Then he waited.

In the bunkhouse Butts and Cory each satisfied himself likewise that his weapons were in good condition.

Butts was the first to emerge. He wanted that five thousand dollars very badly; but Cory Blaine was more interested in having Mason out of the way; and if Butts wanted to take the risk, he could have the five thousand. Neither man knew that Kay White had been to the corral and warned their quarry; and so it was with considerable confidence that they advanced, Blaine a little to the rear and to Butts' left.

The latter was a hundred feet from the stable door when Marvel stepped out into the open. Without a word, without warning, Butts drew and fired. Marvel had drawn one of his guns before stepping from the stables, but his arm had been hanging at his right side and the weapon concealed from the two men by his body. As Butts drew, Mason fired from the hip. Then Blaine fired as Butts stumbled forward, a bullet through his forehead. Blaine missed and Mason fired again.

At the sound of the first shot, the guests had poured from their rooms onto the veranda. Birdie Talbot went into hysterics; and as Blaine crumpled to Mason's second shot, Olga Gunderstrom screamed and fainted. Kay stood tense and white, her hands clenched, her nails biting into her palms. She kept repeating to herself, "He lives! He lives!"

Mason stood now with a gun in each hand. His attitude was defiant as he looked about him for other possible enemies. And then two men rode into the yard. They came at a gallop, for they heard the shots.   At a glance they took in the scene by the corral.   One of the men was elderly. It was the younger who drew his gun.   Buck Mason leaped back into the stables just as the man fired, the bullet burying itself in the door frame in front of which Mason had been standing but an instant before.

"Put up your gun, sheriff," said the older man. "I'll get him without no gunplay."   He rode slowly toward the stables.   "It's all up, Buck," he called.   "Limber up your artillery and come on out.   I'll see you get a square deal."

Instantly Mason stepped from the doorway. "Why the gunplay?" he demanded.

"You're under arrest, Buck," said the older man.   "Let me have your guns."

"What you arrestin' me for, boss?" asked Buck.

"For killin' old man Gunderstrom," replied the sheriff of Comanche County; "but I won't never believe you done it, Buck.   How-some-ever I got a warrant for your arrest and the law's the law."

Mason unbuckled his cartridge belt and handed it up to the sheriff, the two guns hanging in their holsters.

"Tie up your horses and come up to the house," said Buck. "I got a long story to tell and there's others besides you I want to have hear it. Incidental-like, boss, I got the gang that killed Gunderstrom."

"Who done it?" asked the sheriff of Comanche County.

Mason pointed at Blaine, lying in the dust of the ranch yard.

"You'll have hard work provin' that, young feller," said the other man.

"Who the hell are you anyway?" demanded Buck.

"This is the sheriff of Porico County, Buck," explained the older man.

"O.K.," said Mason.

As the three men walked toward the house, a body of horsemen approached the ranch from the south, riding down the Mill Creek trail. Those in the lead saw a man on foot running toward the brush along the river. In a cow country a man on foot is always an object of suspicion. When he is caught running for cover, he is already convicted, even though no one may be aware that a crime has been committed.

The result was that instantly the men rode forward to intercept the lone pedestrian. As they approached him he stopped, for he could not possibly have reached the brush ahead of them. He turned and faced them.

"Who are you and what's your hurry?" demanded one of the men.

"I come out to meet you fellers," said Eddie, his brain spurred to unwonted activity by stress of circumstances. "Buck Mason, the guy that killed old man Gunderstrom over in New Mexico, is down at the stables and two of the fellers are tryin' to get him. There's been some shootin', but I couldn't see what happened."

"A couple of you fellows bring this guy in," said the deputy sheriff of Porico County, "and the rest of you come along with me."

And so it was that the deputy sheriff and his posse galloped into the ranch yard just as Buck and the two sheriffs ascended the steps to the veranda.

"Hello, sheriff," called the deputy to his chief. "You got your man?"

"You bet," exclaimed the sheriff of Porico County. "You know me. I always get my man.

This is the feller that killed old man Gunderstrom over in Comanche County and run off with Mr. White's gal here. I reckon he's the head of this here gang that's been raisin' hell in New Mexico and Arizona for the past year."

XXIII

THE BRASS HEART

Olga Gunderstrom had fully regained consciousness before Buck and the sheriffs ascended the veranda steps. The reaction to the nervous ordeal through which she had passed had left her silent and exhausted, and she sat now staring with wide eyes at the man who had been her childhood playmate and who she now believed to be the slayer of her father. She saw the slender, blond-haired girl in blue overalls come forward and take Buck Mason's hand. "I'm so glad they did not kill you," she heard her say.

"After you came to the corral and told me, there couldn't anybody have killed me," he said in a whisper that not even Olga Gunderstrom could hear.

"Who's this girl?" demanded the sheriff of Porico County.

"She is my daughter," replied John White.

"The girl that was kidnaped?" demanded the sheriff.

"Yes."

"And hobnobbin' with the man that kidnaped her?" demanded the sheriff.

"Don't be foolish," said Kay. "This man did not kidnap me. Two men named Mart and Eddie took me away from Cory Blaine, but I have learned since that the whole thing was arranged by Blaine. This man risked his life many times to ride after me and save me from them. Even Eddie will testify to that. Where is he, father?"

Olga Gunderstrom shrank fearfully into her chair; but almost immediately she regained something of her self assurance, since she was confident that Eddie had made good his escape.

"Why there comes Eddie now," exclaimed John White. "How did he get out of the office?"

"That must have been Eddie we picked up on our way in," said the deputy sheriff of Porico County. "He sure was hot footin' it for parts unknown. Bring him up here, boys," he called to the men escorting Eddie. "We want to talk to that young feller."

When Eddie came onto the porch, Buck Mason turned toward him. "Remember what I told you, Eddie," he said.

"Shut up," snapped the sheriff of Porico County. "Don't you try to influence no witness around here."

"I was just remindin' Eddie to tell the truth," said Mason. "Sometimes it aint so easy for him to remember that."

"Eddie," asked Kay, "who persuaded you to help to kidnap me?"

Eddie looked about as though searching for someone. His eyes finally came to rest on Mason's face. "He didn't get the drop on you; so he must be dead," he said.

"Yes, he is dead," replied Mason.

"Go on, answer the young lady's question," urged the sheriff of Porico County. "Who persuaded you to kidnap her?"

"Cory Blaine," replied Eddie.

"Didn't this feller, Buck Mason, have a hand in it?" demanded the sheriff.

"Naw," said Eddie. "He come after us. Hi Bryam tried to kill him and Hi is dead. Then Mart tried to beat him to the draw and Mart's dead. The only kidnapin' he done was when he kidnaped her away from us."

"Well, maybe he didn't kidnap the gal," said the sheriff of Porico County. "Leastways, we don't seem to have much of a case agin him now; but he killed old man Gunderstrom, and I want you folks here to bear witness that I took him single-handed and that I'm entitled to all the reward."

"Before you spend any of it, I want you to listen to me for a minute," said Mason. "I got to tell my story in court anyway, and maybe it seems a waste of time to tell it now; but there's reasons why I want some of these people here to know the truth." He turned to the sheriff of Comanche County. "May I tell it, boss?" he asked.

"Sure, Buck, hop to it," replied the older man.

"In the first place," said Mason, "for the benefit of those of you who don't know it, I am deputy sheriff of Comanche County in New Mexico."

"That's right," said the sheriff. "He's my chief deputy."

"The afternoon of the night Gunderstrom was killed I rode up to his shack to talk about a line fence that's been a matter of dispute between our families for twenty years. I couldn't get any satisfaction out of the old man, but we did not quarrel. There wasn't enough at stake there anyway to furnish a reasonable cause for me to kill him, and there was another good reason why I couldn't have killed Gunderstrom." He glanced at Olga. "Me and his daughter was playmates ever since we were kids. I liked her better than anybody else I knew. I couldn't have killed her paw.

"When the murder was reported and the boss sent me over to investigate, I seen three things that interested me. There were signs at the tie rail that five horses had been tied there the night before. There were foot prints of five men; two of 'em easy to identify again. One fellow had a heart shaped piece of metal set in the bottom of each heel of his boots, and that heart left a plain imprint in the soft ground. Another one of 'em had the biggest feet I ever seen on a man.

"Then I went into the house. The first thing I seen was one of Ole's' boots lyin' in front of the cot, like it had been kicked around. I examined it very carefully and I seen the imprint of that metal heart on it where the murderer had stepped real heavy on the boot, like he stumbled on it first and then, in trying to catch himself, had stamped down real heavy on it. Did you save that boot, boss, as I asked you to?"

"Yes, I saved it; and we seen that heart shaped mark on it," replied the sheriff.

"Of course the coroner saved the bullet that killed Gunderstrom, too, didn't he?"

"Yes."

"What caliber was it?"

"Forty-five."

"And you know, boss, that I've always packed my old man's forty-fours ever since he died, don't you?"

"Yes, I told them that," replied the sheriff of Comanche County. "They don't nobody think you done it down there, Buck, except Olga Gunderstrom."

"There was another thing I forgot to tell you," continued Mason. "The hoof prints of the horses showed that one of 'em had a big piece broken out of the inside of the off hind hoof, which made it mighty easy to track.

"They rode awful fast and I never did get within sight of 'em, but I could follow 'em easy by that broken hoof; and whenever they dismounted, I seen the heart shaped imprint of that feller's heel, and I noticed that it was always beside the horse with the broken hoof; so I figured that that was his horse; and then old big foot always showed up too whenever they dismounted.

"I trailed 'em right down to the town on the railroad here; and then I got to makin' inquiries there and I heard about this feller Cory Blaine and his dude ranch, and somebody told me that he just come in from his mine the day before. This feller that told me said that Blaine sure was a hard rider, that his horse was about used up when he come through town.

"Still I didn't think I had enough to go on, and I wanted to be sure; so I cached my saddle and bridle, hopped the train to Denver and telegraphed this feller Blaine for accommodations on his dude ranch. As soon as I got word from him that he could take care of me I shaved off my mustache, buys a lot of funny clothes that I had seen pictures of in magazines, and comes down here to the TF, expectin' to clean up everything in a couple of days; but it wasn't so easy. There wasn't nobody with a heart shaped piece of metal in the heel of his boot. There wasn't nobody with the biggest feet in the world, and there wasn't no horse with a broken hoof.

"The first clue I got, and it was a darn slim one at that, was when Dora Crowell and Blaine were discussin' the news that had just come to the ranch that I had been accused of Gunderstrom's murder. Do you remember, Dora, that you said I must be a terrible man because I shot Mr. Gunderstrom right through the heart while he was lyin' asleep on his bed?"

Dora nodded. "Yes," she said, "I remember."

"And then Blaine spoke up and says, 'Between the eyes;' and you said, 'It didn't say that in the paper.'

"That gave me my first hunch that Cory Blaine knew too much about the murder, and so I made up my mind that I'd have to hang around and get to the bottom of it. The next day we goes on a lion hunt; and still there wasn't any boots with hearts on 'em, or big feet, or broken hoofs; but when we got up to Hi Bryam's shack and I seen Hi Bryam and his feet and seen how chummy he and Blaine and Butts were, I commenced to have hopes again.

"Bryam wasn't very chummy with me; but I finally managed to sit down beside him on the step of his cabin one evenin' and put my foot down alongside of his, and there was just the same difference that I'd measured between the length of my foot and the length of the big print around Gunderstrom's cabin, about an inch and a half I should say.

"Then the last night we was up to Bryam's I overheard a conversation between Blaine and Bryam and Butts that gave me an idea that the three of 'em were workin' together on some crooked deal."

He turned to Mr. White. "It was a good thing I overheard that conversation, Mr. White, because, while I didn't know it at the time, it was the outline of a part of the scheme to kidnap Kay. It give me just the clue I needed to follow them.

"I was gettin' closer now, but I didn't have

anything to pin on Blaine, although I was dead sure he was the murderer. I knew that the boss here would save the bullet that killed Gunderstrom. As you all know, the rifling in the barrel of any weapon makes a distinguishing mark upon the bullet that aint like the marks that the rifling in any other weapon makes on its bullet; so I was particularly anxious to get hold of a bullet that had been fired from Blaine's gun. I done that one night by asking him to let me shoot at a target and then, being a tenderfoot," he grinned, "I accidentally fired the gun into my bedroll. I got the bullet here now for comparison when you get back home, boss."

"Good," said the sheriff.

"About this time sombody dropped a remark about Blaine's horse droppin' dead from exhaustion after he come in from his last trip; and, of course, that made me want to see that particular horse pretty bad; so I started talkin' about horse's teeth." He looked at Dora Crowell and grinned again.

"I got to figuring that you weren't as crazy as you tried to make out," said the girl, "but you had me fooled for a while."

"If Cory Blaine had been as bright as you, Dora, I never would have caught him.

"What I wanted particular though was a heel print with a heart in it. Blaine never wore but one pair of boots, and they was just ordinary boots with nuthin' fancy about 'em. I made up my mind that he'd just have to change his boots, and so the night before we got back from the lion hunt I threw one of his boots into the campfire while he was asleep and made believe I'd thrown it at a coyote who had probably ran off with it."

He looked almost shyly at Kay White. "Some folks thought it was a mean thing to do," he continued, "but they didn't know why I done it. Well, the next day after we gets back to the TF Ranch Blaine comes out with an old pair of boots on. They'd been a awful fancy pair of boots in their day, with different colored patent leather trimmin' and sure enough brass hearts set right in the bottom of the heels. It was right then I beat it for town and sent that letter to you, boss.

"I had two of 'em now; and I was pretty sure of Butts, because he was an ornery sort of a cuss anyway, and him and Blaine was mighty thick. Then some time about this time comes a letter tellin' about this feller with a harelip callin' up on the telephone and sayin' that it was Buck Mason that killed Ole Gunderstrom. There wasn't nobody around with a harelip; so I just sort of forgot that for awhile; but I still wanted to see that horse that Blaine rode to death, and so I got Bud to take me to it the day the rest of you folks rode over to Crater Mountain and sure enough there was a piece broken out of the inside of the off rear hoof. I was sure right then that I had Blaine tied up, and I was only waitin' for the sheriff to come when this here kidnapin' blew everything to pieces.

"But in a way it helped, too, for it give me a line on the other two guys, Mart and Eddie. I spotted Eddie the same day Bud took me huntin' horses' teeth. I seen Cory Blaine ridin' over the hills to the west; and after I was able to shake Bud, I followed him and seen him talkin' to two fellers down in the dry gulch on the other side of the hills.

"I wanted a closer view of those two fellers, and so I beat it around to the mouth of the can-

yon when they started down and met 'em there."
He turned to Eddie. "Do you remember, Eddie?" he asked.

The prisoner nodded sullenly. "Yes, I remember," he said.

"I pretended I was a dude and that I was lost,
and when this guy Eddie speaks to me I was
pretty sure that I had number four and that
probably the other feller was number five, for
Eddie sure talked like he has a harelip. He
just got about half his tongue shot away once.
He told me about it in camp yesterday.

"In fact Eddie told me a lot of things. Some
of 'em I'd rather not tell to all of you; but the
five of 'em, Blaine, Butts, Bryam, Mart, and
Eddie was the gang that's been raisin' all this
hell around here for the past year. They were
with Blaine when he went up to kill Ole Gunderstrom. They had no part in the actual killing,
though they were in the cabin when Blaine went
in and shot Ole."

Olga Gunderstrom rose from her chair and
came up to Eddie. She stood directly in front
of him and seized him by the shoulders, her eyes
blazing into his. "Is that the truth?" she de-

manded through clenched teeth, shaking him viciously.

"Leave me go," he cried. "I didn't do it."

"Is Buck Mason telling the truth?" she demanded. "That's what I asked you."

"Yes, he's tellin' the truth," said Eddie sullenly.

"I don't believe you," she cried. "It was Buck Mason that killed my father. Why should this man Blaine have wanted to kill him? He didn't even know him."

"Because your old man was trying to double-cross him," said Eddie. "He handled the stock that we rustled, and we used to cache a lot of the money at one of his ranches here in Arizona. He double-crossed us and wouldn't never give us our share of what he got on the horses and cattle we rustled; and then, just before Blaine croaked him, he comes to this ranch that I'm tellin' you about here in Arizona and swipes most of the money we got hid there; and that's why Cory Blaine killed him, if you want to know."

Olga Gunderstrom swayed slightly and Mason stepped to her side to support her. "Don't touch me," she said. Then she steadied herself and walking slowly from among them, entered the house.

"I'm sorry that happened," said Mason. "That is what I did not want to tell.

"I guess that's about all," said Mason in conclusion. "Some of you folks have been mighty nice to me, and I wanted you to know the truth. You see I really felt worse about them funny pants and the boot garters than I did about being accused of killin' a man; for I knew that I could clear myself from the latter in court, but I might never live down the other."

The sheriff of Porico County cleared his throat. "I reckon we'll be goin', sheriff," he said. "I guess you can take care of the prisoners all right, can't you?"

"You take this Eddie with you, and I'll take care of Buck. I reckon that indictment against him will be quashed at the preliminary hearing."

"I reckon so," said the sheriff of Porico County, "but he'll have to appear here at the coroner's inquest on the shootin' of these four hombres. I'll see that he aint delayed none, though. Good-bye."

"Thanks, Sheriff," said Mason.

"What do you want to do now, Buck?" asked the sheriff of Comanche County. "Start for town now or wait till the cool of the evening?"

"I want to go to bed," said Mason. "I aint slept for two nights."

"Just a moment, Mason," said John White; "I'd like a word with you."

Mason turned and faced him. "Sure, sir," he said; "what do you want?"

"I want to apologize."

"That aint necessary," Mason assured him.

"I think it is."

Mason shook his head. "Blaine was pretty slick," he said. "Most anybody might have believed that story of his. I don't blame you none for not believin' me. That was about the slickest alibi and frame-up I ever heard. There was just one thing wrong with it."

"What was that?" asked White.

"His aim," said Mason.

White smiled in understanding.

"You seem to have handled this whole thing in an extremely clever manner, Mason," said White.

"It's the slickest piece of detective work I ever

seen," said the Sheriff of Comanche County, "but he comes by it natural. His old man was the best sheriff Comanche or any other county ever had."

"He's done a fine piece of work for law, order, and justice," said White; "and while the size of the reward may not be commensurate with the obligation society and I owe him, it will not be inconsiderable."

"What do you mean?" asked Mason.

"The reward I promised for the safe return of Kay," replied White.

Mason's eyes hardened. "I aint aimin' to collect no reward, mister." This was the fighting deputy of Comanche County speaking.

White flushed, but he held out his hand. "I understand," he said, "but in fairness to me you should let me do something — anything you ask."

"I'll be askin' something later, I hope," replied Mason, his eyes softening.

White smiled. "I hope so, too, my boy," he said; "and now go on to bed."

Before he turned in, Buck Mason cut a new notch on each of his father's forty-fours.

He was up early the next morning, for it does not take youth long to recuperate; and, furthermore, he was ravenously hungry. As he stepped out onto the veranda in the cool, fresh air of the morning, he saw a girl walking toward the river, a girl that he might not have recognized except for the blond head; for the lithe body was clothed in smart sport togs, which reminded him of illustrations he had seen in *Vogue;* but too often had he watched the sunlight playing in that blond hair to fail to recognize it, whatever the apparel of its owner. So he, too, hastened down toward the river.

Cottonwoods grow along the river, hiding much of the view from the veranda; but they do not hide everything; and when, a few minutes later, Dora Crowell stepped out of the TF Ranch house to fill her lungs with the early morning air, she caught a glimpse of a figure standing among the cottonwoods by the river; and when she looked more closely and saw that the one figure was really two, she smiled and turned her eyes in another direction.

THE END